A Spy
in Old
West Point

By ANNE EMERY
Illustrated by Lorence F. Bjorklund

In this, the fourth of her "Spy" books, the author has chosen a historical episode from the Revolutionary War. It involves a real spy—Major André. The fictional hero, Jock Fraser, is given an important part in his apprehension.

All the major events in the book are historically accurate, and all of the military officers really were on the scene, as the book describes. The only fictional characters involved in this exciting story are Jock, his gunsmith father, their family, and a few friends.

Jock has come to know Major André and to like him. Readers of A Spy in Old West Point will sympathize with Jock's dilemma: if he helps Major André escape, he will collect enough money to fulfill his own ambitions and free his father from debt; but to help André, Jock will have to violate what he knows to be his patriotic duty.

A Spy in Old West Point is, first of all, an engrossing story. It is also an excellent way of absorbing information about an important episode in American history, and of learning many fascinating facts about guns and gunmaking.

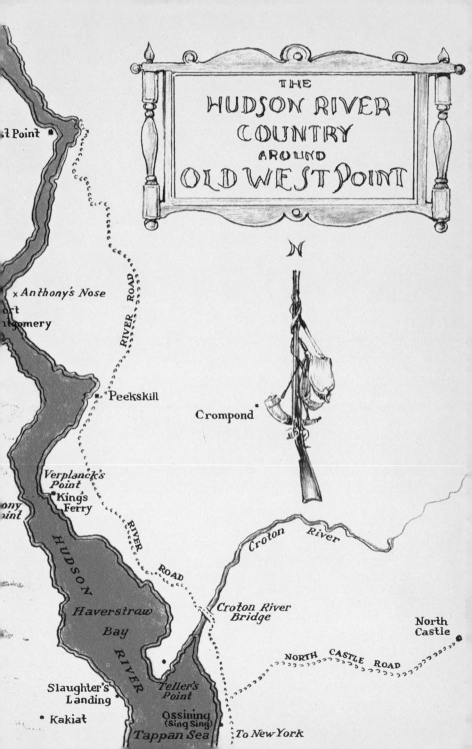

A Spy in
Old West Point

A Spy in
Old West Point

By ANNE EMERY
Illustrated by Lorence F. Bjorklund

Rand McNally & Company
Chicago · New York · San Francisco

Other books by Anne Emery:

A SPY IN OLD NEW ORLEANS
Illustrated by Emil Weiss

A SPY IN OLD PHILADELPHIA
Illustrated by H. B. Vestal

A SPY IN OLD DETROIT
Illustrated by H. B. Vestal

Chapter 1

THE Hudson River rolled dark and sluggish beneath the black-clouded skies, and the thunder pounded through the granite walls like a bouncing cannon ball.

Jock Fraser scowled up at the sky. "You'd think the Redcoats were firing right down the river from Verplanck's Point at us," he said to his father. "Mebbe they will be, too. Any day now."

Jock was a well-built lad of fourteen, stocky and strong for his age, with the red hair of his Scottish forebears, clear blue eyes, and a wide mouth that pushed forward when he was sulky. He felt sulky quite often these days. But who wouldn't be out of humor, with the British having taken King's Ferry three weeks ago? They were now settled in and holding the lower Hudson River, clear to New York City.

The thunder rolled down the valley again, and the June day darkened swiftly. Jock's father looked up from the gunlock he was testing. It was only three in the afternoon, and the sudden eerie darkness seemed like a warning.

"We'll get back to the house," he said. "Something's going to happen."

The men put aside their work, banked the forge fires, and began to run across the farmyard, where chickens, thinking it was night, scattered before them, and where potato plants, carrot tops, and green onion leaves were streaming in the rising wind. It was June 20, 1779.

"Jock!" his father called, "fetch the cow to the barn. Lightning might strike her under that tree!"

The boy ran toward the fenced pasture and pulled on the cow. She was unwilling to hurry, and he bawled and shoved at her while his father shouted, "This is the kind of weather when the Cowboys might cross the river and pick her up. Lock the door!"

As Jock nudged the cow into the barn and locked the door behind her, the clouds opened and the rain dropped in a sudden torrent. The lightning stabbed through the clouds, and in its momentary brightness Jock could see the trees tossing wildly in the wind that howled through the river walls and roared across the highlands. He cringed in spite of himself at the exploding thunder as he ran toward the house. It sounded as if the earth were splitting behind him.

Another flash illuminated the world, and in its brilliance a rider, crouched low on his horse, charged up to the white picket fence along the road in front of the house, and pulled his horse to a shuddering stop.

The boy ran for the kitchen door. You couldn't take

6

A rider, crouched low on his horse, charged up to the fence

a chance on anyone who turned up these days. A family down the road had let in a stranger a month ago, and he had turned out to be a Tory militiaman who robbed and beat the family and fired the house. Jock ducked into the family kitchen and called, "There's someone at the front door." He picked up his musket from the corner before he finished the sentence. His sister, Peggy, sitting at the spinning wheel, stopped the treadle with her hand on the big wheel and looked up at Jock. She was thirteen, red-haired and demure.

George Fraser had already opened the door, and an officer in an American uniform was accompanying him to the kitchen as Jock spoke.

"I'll never get used to the weather in this valley," the officer grumbled, as he shook his hat so that water flew across the brick floor. "I can't even find the road to the ferry in this storm."

George Fraser eyed him skeptically. "King's Ferry?"

"That's where I'm going, to cross over to the American side."

George grunted acquiescence, but he said nothing. Jock knew exactly what his Pa was thinking. A man approaching Verplanck's Point, where King's Ferry crossed the river, must belong to the British.

The officer said lightly, "Certainly the British will not refuse transport to someone who carries a flag . . ."

"Humph," Fraser snorted. "Well, sit down. It'll be some time yet before this storm blows out."

The officer sat down, looking not at all self-conscious. "You are Patriots, then?" he asked.

"Oh, I'm not saying that." The Frasers were cautious about expressing their loyalties. You had to be, when the nearest neighbors were Tories, and you never knew whether a Patriot or a Tory was knocking at your door. If you declared the wrong cause, you could be dragged out of your house and tarred and feathered, or have the house burned over your head. Who knew whether this officer might not have a band of soldiers hidden outside?

Jock was studying the expression of their guest. He could not tell much about the man: good-looking, youngish, with a mouth that looked impatient and determined. But it was the eyes that caught his attention. While the officer was speaking in a friendly, informal tone, his eyes, steel-gray, hard and unsmiling, were noticing everything. Uniforms did not prove much these days.

The British officers were not so bad. Mostly they were polite and even friendly, as if, when this war was won, they hoped the Americans would like them. But the volunteer militia pillaged everything with a vengeful spite that made the Hudson Valley people fear them more than the entire British army. And they wore any captured uniforms they picked up.

"Well, perhaps your loyalties are with the British?" the officer said, in a tone that demanded an answer.

George Fraser shook his head. "We don't take sides in this war," he muttered, looking around for his pipe and busying himself with lighting it. "All we want is to be let alone."

Mrs. Fraser snatched a pot of boiling water from the crane.

"Sir, surely you will have a little food and a cup of coffee before you go on your way?"

His penetrating gray eyes contemplated her for a moment. And for that moment Jock saw his mother as the stranger saw her: young, vivacious and pretty, in a pink dress with a wide ruffled collar and flowered overskirt. She had had that dress since the war began over four years ago and now, in 1779, it was still one of Jock's favorites.

"Coffee?" the officer said in a questioning tone. "That would be fine. And I think your bread must be good, Mrs. Fraser. I was looking for a place to dine when the storm caught me."

Maggie Fraser poured out a cup of fragrant coffee and set out cream and sugar, bread and butter, and applesauce. The officer ate with relish, and the atmosphere seemed to lighten.

"Your New York apples are the best I ever found," he commented, spooning out the third dishful of applesauce.

"And where else have you eaten apples?" Maggie Fraser asked, smiling at him coquettishly.

He settled back in the wooden armchair, looking contented. "I've spent a lot of time in Philadelphia." Jock's mouth hardened. The British had occupied Philadelphia up until a year ago. "Their apples are not the same at all," the officer said.

Then he sat up in a businesslike manner. "Mrs. Fraser, I think we can talk openly now."

"Me?" Maggie Fraser looked startled and affronted.

He laughed. "Why don't you tell me the truth? You're Patriots in this house."

"Now look here!" George Fraser sprang to his feet and shook his pipe threateningly at their guest. "You got no call to be deciding things like that! I told you we're as neutral as a body can be in these times. Who are you, sir? We don't talk openly with any stranger."

"Captain McLane, in General Washington's service, sir." The officer waved his hand indifferently. "I respect your caution. But when Mrs. Fraser offered coffee I knew I was in a Patriot house. I've drunk tea in many a Loyalist house since the war began. But never in a Patriot house."

Jock's mouth fell open.

Captain Allen McLane was one of his heroes. He was one of General Washington's most efficient spies, and for that very reason you didn't hear much about him. But everybody knew he had frightened the British out of their wits with bombs, during a celebration party for General Howe, back there in Philadelphia. And everyone knew he had got the information General Washington needed for some of his most successful assaults.

"This is my purpose," McLane was saying. "This country around here is desolate and dangerous. And yet the Hudson Valley is perhaps the most important line of defense in our entire war plan. If we lose the Hudson River, we lose the war. It's as simple as that."

"I don't mind saying we don't want to see the Americans lose the Hudson," Mr. Fraser conceded, chewing on the stem of his pipe. He was still being cautious about his loyalties.

McLane nodded. "Good enough. What we need in these parts is a line of communication. I'd like to leave a letter here, for someone who will come by to pick it up. I can't tell you who he'll be, or when he'll come. But if he says something about the Liberty Tree, let him come in. That is the password. He'll know where to look."

He glanced around the kitchen. It was a large room, with a heavy trestle table in the middle of the brick floor, stools at the table, a couple of heavy chairs near the hearth. The big stone fireplace was hung about with cooking utensils and fire tools. A finely carved and decorated bellows leaned in the corner of the hearth, and above the fireplace on the stone mantel were a couple of candle molds, some pewter candlesticks, and three tankards. Captain McLane got up and moved about the room, studying it carefully. A picture of Mrs. Fraser, done by a wandering artist, hung near the small-paned window that looked out on the farmyard. A tall clothes press stood in the corner.

The captain stopped beside the fireplace.

"When someone comes by and gives the password," he repeated, and Jock, watching him narrowly, saw a scrap of paper drop into the bellows, as if unintentionally, "take him in. He'll know where to find the message. This will be a great help to us."

He swung about and faced them again, smiling warmly. "It's hard enough to get word from the general's headquarters to the officers out in the field—especially here in the valley, where the people's loyalties are so divided. Part of my work has been to discover Patriots who would work with us and be trustworthy enough to let no one know."

George Fraser swept his family with a stern look.

"No one in this house knows anything about this!" he announced, as if he were barking an order. "Nothing, you all understand? Except the password. Peggy?" His daughter nodded, looking a little scared. "Jock?" Jock nodded vigorously, pleased all the way through that he could thus work for the Patriots. "Maggie?" His wife gave a dignified nod.

The gunsmith turned to Captain McLane. "You can count on this house, Captain."

"My thanks to you all." Captain McLane smiled from one to another. "I don't know when I'll be coming this way again. But be assured that you are helping the American cause."

He looked out of the window. None of them had

noticed that the darkness had vanished, the skies had cleared, and a pale ray of sunlight lay across the floor from the west window.

"I'll be on my way now," he said, striding to the door. "Don't come out. Do nothing to call attention to my leaving."

While they watched, he opened the door as silently as if it had opened itself, glanced out, and up and down the road. And then, swiftly, he flung the horse's rein from the hitching post, leaped astride, and was gone into the sunlight that flickered through the trees upon the road, so quickly that Jock had the eerie feeling that he might never have been there at all.

Peggy flopped down upon the settle and cried, "Well, of all things! But isn't he a handsome Patriot?"

"Never mind," her mother said, moving about the kitchen poking up the fire and setting the dishes from the table on the shelf for washing. "Just don't say anything about this afternoon to anyone, Peggy."

George Fraser went out the back door, calling, "Jock? Let's finish that gun now."

"I'm coming. One minute."

Jock sauntered about the kitchen, stopping by the fire to gaze into the kettle hanging from the crane. While the women had their backs turned, he glanced into the bellows. The folded edge of a white paper was barely visible. Satisfied, he turned and started for the forge.

Chapter 2

THE Fraser homestead stood in a spot on the Croton River, near Teller's Point. George Fraser had settled there fifteen years before, when he had first come from Scotland, because Oliver Cartwright, who made the best iron for gun barrels in the state of New York, wanted a gunsmith on his iron plantation, and the gunsmith had needed water power.

George Fraser was now known as one of the finest gunsmiths in the Hudson Valley and he was teaching his craft to his two sons. Jock's older brother, Rob, had been a skilled apprentice, about to become a journeyman gunsmith. But two months before, as soon as the spring planting was done, he had run off and enlisted in the Patriot army.

Jock was doing as much as he could to take Rob's place. But one apprentice was not enough, and it was hard to find apprentices these days. Most of them wanted to work in the cities, where there was lots of excitement and, thus far, George Fraser had been unable to find one to replace Rob.

Almost all of the land on that side of the Hudson

had belonged to great land-owning families for generations. George Fraser's greatest ambition was to own, free and clear, his own small patch of ground. But no matter how much money he made he could not buy the ground he lived on, because Oliver Cartwright refused to sell any part of his hundred thousand acres. In the meantime, George had to pay his landlord what amounted to a third of his income as annual rent for the land where he had his home and his forge.

But now that the colonies were at war, there was little use of thinking about anything but keeping up with the day-to-day demands for new guns, the repairing of old guns, trying to get deliveries of gunlocks, and finding the money to pay for the coal for the forge. Prices were rising constantly, and paper money seemed to be worth less each time the bill collector came around.

When the war was over, George Fraser told his son over and over, things would be different. Jock thought the war had been going on practically forever, and it didn't look to him as if it would ever be over.

Above the Croton River the American armies still held most of the ground along the Hudson, although the loss of Stony Point and King's Ferry had been a staggering blow. Below Tarrytown, New York State was in the hands of the British. Between Tarrytown and the Croton River was the Neutral Ground, where bands of ravaging militia roamed the countryside, driving off cattle and horses for both British and American armies, and often

Jock sighed heavily, grabbing a cleaning rod

enough for themselves; stealing money and food; and murdering in their homes families on lonely farms. It was worse, now that the British held King's Ferry.

The day following Captain McLane's visit was sunny and clear, and Jock could see the tiny red-coated figures moving about the works at King's Ferry, far up the river. He glared at them angrily, wishing he could be in the army, fighting them.

His father broke into his thoughts: "There's work to be done, Jock. Don't just stand there mooning!"

Jock sighed heavily, grabbing a cleaning rod and

thrusting it into a rusty musket barrel with such energy that it bent in his hand. He had to pull it out and straighten it, and his father looked at him, disgusted with such clumsy work.

But Jock was filled with exasperation this morning, and working on a beaten-up, badly made old gun was no help. He wanted to slam and throw something.

"Enough of that nonsense!" his father barked at him, as the gun clattered on the stone floor. "You're always talking about wanting to help the Patriots. You can help them more by fixing these guns for them than by running out to fight. Half their trouble comes from men, who should be staying home and supplying the armies, running around calling for guns to fight with, when there aren't enough guns. Nor apprentices, either!" he added angrily.

"Be a good thing if Rob came home for the winter," George Fraser muttered to himself, as he pounded on a crooked musket barrel. "They can't keep the men warm. Can't feed 'em. Ought to let 'em all go home and work during the winter."

George Fraser had strong opinions on how the war should be conducted. But since neither General Clinton of the British forces, nor General Washington with the American armies was fighting the way Fraser recommended, he had stopped expecting good sense from the military.

Jock straightened up and looked up-river toward King's

Ferry again. He wondered if Captain McLane had crossed last night as he had planned. He wondered what the captain was trying to find out in this part of the valley, and he recalled his words: ". . . the most important line of defense in the entire war plan. . ."

George Fraser mopped his forehead and sat down for a moment to look at the river, shining in the bright day. Keeping up with army contracts kept a man working all day long until sundown these days, and still he fell behind.

A rider swung off the main road and cantered down the lane to the forge. "Messenger from quartermaster," he said. "Guns ready?" He showed his credentials and dismounted. He was no older than Rob, but he looked thin and hard, with hollows of fatigue or starvation under his eyes.

"It's getting on for supper time," George said. "Come along and have a good meal. We can always feed a hungry soldier."

"I don't mind if I do," the boy said. "I can always use a bit of food, and a drink for the Liberty Tree."

Jock heard the password, and all his muscles tightened. But his father didn't seem to notice anything at all. The messenger stepped outside the forge and looked around. Then he fastened his horse in a spot behind the forge, where it would be concealed from the road.

"Truth to tell, there's never enough to eat in that army," he said frankly. "I dunno why they can't get the supplies to the men. Half the time we're living off the country, and—" he glanced at Fraser "—we know that's hard on the people."

Near the door to the kitchen Peggy was washing clothes and sheets. She was a lovely girl, with her red curls, teasing blue eyes, and freckles on her fair skin that worried her, and she made a pretty picture with her skirts tucked up and suds to her elbows. Although she was only thirteen, she seemed to be already grown up.

The messenger noticed her with approval, but she took no notice. The men moved along the path to the door. When they entered the kitchen, Jock saw their guest looking around the room quickly and intently. Then he sagged into one of the chairs. Mrs. Fraser stood beside him, leaning on the table. "I'm Maggie Fraser. You're from the American army?"

"Yes, ma'am. I'm from the army, the one that fights for the Liberty Tree. Name of Benjamin."

Maggie smiled at him, as if he were Rob come home. "Seems as if the best thing we can do for that Liberty Tree is to feed the men who are fighting for it."

She brought out a bowl of chicken stew, bread and butter, a tankard of ale, a round of cheese. Benjamin fell upon the food as if he were starving. Jock wondered what Rob was getting to eat in the army, and his mother was watching Benjamin with a soft expression, as if she were wondering the same thing.

Benjamin cleaned his plate, drained the tankard of ale, and stretched luxuriously. A smile of pure happiness lit his sunken eyes. Then he got to his feet and began to walk about the kitchen. Talking casually about army life, he picked up the bellows and studied the decoration on it.

"Pretty thing, ain't it?"

"My father made that bellows forty years ago," Maggie told him. "Look at the carving on the handles."

He examined it carefully and set it down again. Jock never did see him take the paper out. Benjamin moved away from the fireplace and leaned on the table.

"Ma'am, I sure hate to leave in a hurry, but I guess it's time to be on the road again. Thank 'ee for the fine meal. Mebbe I can come back and eat another some day." He grinned at her, looking younger than when he came in.

"You go north?" she asked.

"Who, me? Ma'am, I couldn't say."

With his hand on the latch of the kitchen door, he froze. Motioning the Frasers to be silent, he listened alertly. Hoofbeats on the dusty main road were approaching the house and pulling up outside.

George Fraser stepped to the window overlooking the entrance. Jock stood by the window that opened on the laundry yard. A British officer was standing there speaking to Peggy.

Jock waved to Benjamin to move away from the door. The messenger crossed the room on swift silent feet, and stepped inside the clothes press. Maggie Fraser closed the door firmly and turned the latch to hold it shut.

Chapter 3

Watching through the kitchen window, the curtain blowing out away from him, Jock could hear everything in the yard clearly.

"May I water my horse here?" the officer asked Peggy politely.

Peggy looked up at him, laughing flirtatiously, and said, "Why certainly, sir. The trough is right there."

Jock gnawed a fingernail in exasperation.

Until about a year ago, he and his sister had been good friends. But in the past year Peggy had seemed to become older than Jock almost overnight. She had changed from the romping tomboy, who had gone fishing with him, to a demure and coquettish damsel who bored him and who laughed at him too often. He had the disturbing feeling that she was way ahead of him.

So he watched her now, irritated and critical. Why must she be like that with a British officer? Why couldn't she be aloof and stern with the enemy?

The officer stood beside his horse as it drank thirstily.

"It's such a hot day," he said, "and Lady, here, has served me well today." He patted the mare's neck fondly. "I felt the least I could do was give her a cold drink!"

"Of course!" Peggy agreed, her blue eyes sparkling brightly. She laughed a giggly kind of soft laugh that Jock admitted, unwillingly, was very fetching. "And wouldn't you like a cold drink for yourself, sir?" She moved gracefully around the well, and dipped up fresh cold water with the pewter mug sitting on the well's edge. "Our water is supposed to be exceptionally good."

He drank as thirstily as his horse, and handed the cup back to her.

"And so it is." He mopped his forehead. "The weather in your country is incredible."

"I wish you good journey," Peggy said, exactly as if she were inviting him to stay the week.

Suddenly he slapped his pockets and exclaimed, "Your bright eyes have made a dolt of me! I'm looking for Fraser's Forge, and nigh forgot. Can you direct me?"

Her face lighted, and Jock clenched his fists, wishing to shake the silly girl. George Fraser, shaking his head as if he thought his daughter hopelessly foolish, turned and moved toward the door. Jock followed him.

"Why, sir, this is Fraser's Forge!" Peggy cried. She pointed to the sign by the road and giggled again. "Let me call my father."

"Good day, sir. And can I serve you?" George spoke in a neutral tone.

The officer spun around, startled. He was handsome and boyish, with an appealing smile, as if he liked these Americans and hoped they liked him. "Major André, sir, of His Majesty's command. And very grateful for your good well water."

"George Fraser, gunsmith."

"What fortune! I was referred to you, sir, as the finest gunsmith in the state of New York."

The gunsmith was visibly pleased, though he tried not to let it show. "Indeed? And what work have you in mind?"

"My pistol, sir." André pulled out a handsome little silver-mounted pistol and Jock moved closer to see it. "The spark falls short of the priming pan, and I can't tell why."

Fraser turned the little weapon over, cocked it, pulled the trigger. "I think I know what it needs. But it will take a little time."

The officer took a gold watch from his pocket and consulted it. Jock was fascinated in spite of himself. He had seen only two silver watches in all his life, and never a gold one.

"I don't mind waiting, Mr. Fraser. I'm on my way back to New York, and if I don't get the pistol fixed now, I don't know when I could return."

"You have some gunsmiths in New York." Fraser's tone was dry.

"I know." The major's tone matched the gunsmith's. "One of them worked on my pistol a week ago, and it's worse now than before he tampered with it." His voice was persuasive. "If you don't mind my waiting for you to do the job, I don't mind the waiting."

George Fraser turned toward the house, and Jock knew he was trying to suppress a smile. His father smiled fairly seldom. His attitude generally was: "What is there to smile about?" But this young British officer had struck a rare note of sympathy with George Fraser, as well as with Peggy.

"Maggie," her husband said, as he came in the door, "better give that young man something to eat. It won't do any harm to feed a Redcoat now and then." He went back to the door and called into the yard. "Major, you can eat while you're waiting."

The major looked toward the house and smiled like an old friend.

"Very good, sir. I'll just fasten my mare."

Peggy walked beside him as if she were drawn by a magnet, while he fastened the mare in a shady place. Together they came in to the table, where Maggie set out as good a meal as she had served to Benjamin.

"I do regret arriving at your dinner hour, Mrs. Fraser," Major André said. "But I assure you I shall not regret the dinner." He smiled with winning appreciation.

"We have lots of food," Maggie said, setting out bread and butter and ale and cold milk. "You chose a good day." She glanced at him as if she were teasing him. "We're glad to have you join us."

"Shall I tell you how much I hoped you'd invite me to stay?" he asked. "When I smelled that wonderful food I felt heaven had directed me to Fraser's Forge!"

25

"Have you been long in this country, Major?" George Fraser asked.

"Long enough to be almost a colonial," he said. "There is a certain wild attraction about this land of yours that makes one wish sometimes . . ." He did not say what he wished, and Peggy immediately believed he wished to be American.

"Would you wish to be an American?" she demanded eagerly. "I mean, of course, when the war is over?"

He met her eyes gravely. "When the war is over, this will be a great country," he assured her. But he evaded the direct answer she was listening for. "You know—" he sounded nostalgic "—I spent a winter in your great city of Philadelphia. It was probably one of the happiest times of my life."

But that was the wrong note, and Jock scowled. When Major André had spent a winter in Philadelphia, the British were occupying the city.

The major smiled apologetically, knowing at once that he had stepped on sensitive feelings, and he went on in a different vein.

"I knew another Peggy there," he said, lowering his voice to a romantic note. "One of the loveliest ladies I have ever met—and, believe me" —his dark eyes swept the family as if he were including its ladies, too—"I have met many lovely ladies in America. That would be reason enough to stay here the rest of my life."

The ladies laughed with pleasure, and Peggy leaned

across the table. "Would you—are you going back to Philadelphia some day?"

He shook his head, and a mournful expression darkened his eyes for a moment and then gave way to a smile. "She is no longer there, if that is what you mean. She married one of your greatest generals only this past April. She is Mrs. Benedict Arnold now."

"Oh-h-h-" Peggy Fraser breathed a long sigh of romantic sympathy.

"Wait—I have a sketch I made of her once." He drew out a small folder from his pocket, extracted a slip of paper, and handed it to Peggy Fraser. It was a pencil sketch of a girl of about eighteen, with determined eyes and a teasing smile.

"She's beautiful." Peggy sighed. She handed the sketch to Jock, who glanced at it with some interest. Mrs. Benedict Arnold! Then Peggy said, "Oh, Major André! What a lovely picture! Would you make one of me while you're here?"

"I should like that very much," he said gallantly. "You might sit for me while Mr. Fraser is mending my pistol. It will be my pleasure."

Mrs. Fraser set down some trifle for dessert, and Peggy took away the dishes. Then she said, "My brother's in the Continental army. Would it not be a strange thing if you met him some day?"

"Strange indeed." Major André's tone was guarded. "Did he tell you where he's stationed?"

"Not a word." Peggy seemed suddenly to recall where her conversation might lead, and closed her pretty mouth. Then she began on a new line. "And how do you like New York, after Philadelphia, Major André?"

"The people seem happy. Of course you know New York is a Loyalist city."

"We know."

There didn't seem much left to say. Jock felt fidgety about Benjamin, trying to find a question that might lead to information for him. The major finished his dessert, and Peggy jumped up vivaciously. "Do you want to sketch me now?"

He placed her beside a table near the window and took out pencil and paper. For some minutes he sketched, silent and attentive. Jock moved to look over his shoulder. It was fascinating to see the likeness of his sister appear on paper.

The major looked up. "It's finished!"

"Oh, let me see it!" Peggy came over with a skipping step. "I can't wait!" He handed it to her. "Do I really look like that?" She was enormously pleased. "Major André, I like this picture of me as much as the one of the other Peggy!"

He smiled and chucked her under the chin. "There's not so much difference, after all!"

She blushed and retreated. "Might you come back this way some time?"

"I certainly hope to."

For some minutes he sketched, silent and attentive

George Fraser brought in the pistol from the forge. The major checked it carefully; it worked perfectly.

"Excellent, Mr. Fraser. I couldn't be more pleased." He handed the gunsmith a silver coin. "My appreciation for a fine piece of work, and a good meal to boot!"

He mounted his mare, agile and graceful, waved his hat to the Frasers, set it jauntily on his head, and rode south, into the sun, toward New York.

Peggy was staring, rapt, at the sketch he had made. "Wasn't he wonderful?" she demanded.

"Don't be a fool," Jock told her, annoyed with her enthusiasm. "He's a British officer."

"Oh, that doesn't matter," she said airily. "I'll persuade him to come over to the American cause."

She danced into the house on light toes, and her mother laughed. But George Fraser was annoyed.

"The occupation of King's Ferry is no joke, I say. Peggy! Come back here."

She came to the door, being charming. "Did you want me, Father?"

"Just stop mooning about the enemy, and no more jokes about the British, that's what I say."

"Oh, well, of course it was all a joke, and I'll say no more about it!" She sounded agreeable, but she pulled out the sketch again, and looked at it swooningly. Then she winked teasingly at Jock, tucked the precious sketch into the bodice of her dress, and disappeared into the kitchen.

"Girls!" Jock muttered in disgust.

"At that"—his father sounded mollified—"his money is worth more than Continental currency." He pulled out the piece of silver, bit it to test its purity, and put it in another pocket. "That bit of silver will come in handy when paper gets more useless."

Jock went across the room to unlatch the door of the clothes press, and Benjamin poked his head out warily.

"All clear?"

"All clear."

"Did I hear him say he was Major André?" Benjamin asked.

Peggy stiffened at the sink, where she was washing the major's supper dishes with a dreamy expression. She turned to look coldly over her shoulder at the American soldier.

Maggie answered, "That's what he said."

Benjamin scratched his head thoughtfully. "You know, ma'am, Major André helped General Clinton take Stony Point. He's thought to be the best intelligence man in the British command."

"Intelligence? You mean spying?"

"Ma'am, intelligence is the genteel word. Spying is what gets done, when you're finding the information the general wants. And Major André supplies Clinton with what he wants to know about the Hudson Valley. You know which way he rode?"

"He said he was going to New York."

Benjamin moved toward the door as if reluctant to leave. Then he stopped beside Peggy. "Guess you got a pretty memento from the British spy, miss."

She glared at him, and turned her eyes resolutely upon her soapsuds, refusing to look up again. Benjamin grinned, as if her annoyance amused him. "Well, ma'am, I'll be on my way now."

He walked with a jaunty step back to the forge, where he loaded the guns upon his horse, and disappeared down a hidden back lane.

Peggy left her dishpan and sat down on the doorstep, chin on her hands, looking dreamily down the road to New York.

Jock said angrily, "How can you think of a foppish fellow like André? Especially when he's a spy?"

She didn't bother to lift her eyes from the road.

"Your dear Benjamin there is a clod," she said loftily. "Major André is a gentleman."

Jock was so angry he could think of no retort at all, and he turned on his heel and stamped to the forge, where he bent another ramrod.

Chapter 4

FOR the next few weeks the days went by quietly. There was no word from Rob. But the Frasers were used to that silence.

There was no word from Major André. But Peggy talked about him every day, and Jock ignored his sister until his mother scolded him for sulking. She also scolded Peggy for foolish dreaming.

There was no word of fighting. But some gossip went around the valley that the British had withdrawn some of their troops to New York, leaving a garrison to hold the forts at King's Ferry.

The valley was filled with a tense and secret excitement. Something was going to happen, but none knew what. Horsemen rode the lonely roads at night. A stranger stopped by the Frasers' kitchen one night late, mumbled "Liberty Tree," stayed only for a drink of ale, and rode on. Two days later another stranger gave the password, stopped the night, and rode on.

On July 13, an American officer asked for a night's lodging. George Fraser went to the door grumbling, "I'm getting tired of these soldiers thinking you've got nothing to do but wait on them. Who is it?"

"General Anthony Wayne, General Washington's service."

The door swung open, and the travel-worn officer stepped in, looking sharply around. He had an expression of strain, as if he were running against time. Jock met his eyes, and the man stared at him, eyes narrowed, unsmiling. Then he nodded.

"May I have a bed for the night? This is strange territory, and I may have lost my way. In any case, I'd prefer to travel by daylight."

"Certainly, sir. American army around here now?" George asked.

"Coming and going as usual."

Peggy glanced at him indifferently, and Jock resented that. But General Wayne gave her the merest glance, finished the meal Maggie Fraser set before him, asked where he might sleep, and retired early. At the sound of hoofbeats, Jock awoke at dawn, and sprang out of bed to look out of the window. General Wayne was riding up the river road toward Verplanck's Point.

At breakfast Peggy said, "I don't know why the Patriot officers can't be as nice as the British. Do you suppose we'll ever see Major André again?"

"I should hope not!" Jock exploded. "If he's spying for the British, he means trouble."

Unexpectedly, two days later, good news was ringing through the valley. "The Americans have re-taken Stony

Point! Anthony Wayne's troops took it with bayonets! Hardly fired a shot!"

It was ringing in two entirely different tones. Beverly Robinson, the well-known Tory who had left the valley two years before, came riding down the road and stopped to water his horse at the Frasers. Mr. Fraser had made his hunting guns before the war began.

"Mr. Robinson," George Fraser cried, "it's been a long time since you've come by this way."

"Long enough," said Robinson, looking sulky. "I had occasion to collect some papers from my house that the rebels are using, up near West Point . . ." He took a long drink of water from the well and set down the pewter mug hard enough to dent it.

"They're polite enough to the landlord, letting you come and go," George Fraser commented. "And how does your gun work these days?"

"Well enough. When we get rid of the rebels and the country is our own again, I'll bring it in for conditioning, Mr. Fraser. Well—on to Tarrytown. At least that's still our territory."

He struck his spurs into his horse's flanks and galloped on south. George watched him go, a rare grin lighting his face.

"I guess Mr. Robinson isn't so pleased about the rebels taking Stony Point," Jock remarked.

"He's got a nice house up beyond Stony Point, and the

Americans took it, along with the fort. No wonder he's sour," said George.

A rowdy group of rebel soldiers came tramping down the road, singing as they marched and beating the time with their footsteps. They were singing "Liberty Tree" and, as they approached, Jock could hear the final words:

> *From the East to the West blow the trumpet*
> > *to arms,*
> > *Thro' the land let the sound of it flee:*
> > *Let the far and the near all unite with a cheer*
> > *In defense of our Liberty Tree.*

A rowdy group of rebel soldiers came tramping down the road

George Fraser stood up and waved at them from the forge.

"So ye took back Stony Point!" he yelled.

"We took it back!" they chorused. And then the leader bawled, "Give us the new verse for *Yankee Doodle!*" and they began singing again:

> *So now we've taken Stony Point*
> > *With our brave General Wayne, sir,*
> *We fought all night without a shot,*
> > *To hold this ground again, sir!*

Jock sprang to his feet. "I'm going to march along with them, Pa." He ran to catch up, and his father's voice shouted hoarsely after him. In spite of himself, Jock slowed down to hear what his Pa was calling.

"Tell them they're good boys!" his father yelled. "I'll make their bayonets any time!"

Jock caught up with the last of the men on the bridge crossing the Croton.

"Where are we going?" he asked, looking at the dirty, unshaven faces and feeling he was in the company of heroes.

"Nearest tavern we can find. It was a long, thirsty night."

"Are we going to keep Stony Point?"

Three men chorused together, "We'll keep it, boy, and all the rest of this land!"

The big one with the patch on his eye waved his tattered hat and cried, "Let's have *Yankee Doodle* again!"

But Jock was eager for a tale of heroism, and he demanded, "What happened last night?" The men laughed aloud and all began to talk at once.

Then one of them cried, "You tell him, Jake!" and the big man with the patch on his eye told the story. "Well, it was like this. Nobody told us where we was going. But General Wayne started us marching west from camp by noon, and we went all day. Boy, it was hot!" He mopped his forehead in recollection of the heat, and the group slowed their steps to listen to him.

"So about nine in the evening when it's already dark, we come to some farm. You know Mr. Springsteel?"

Jock nodded eagerly, "He's a friend of Pa."

"Our colonel shows us where we're going: and you know Stony Point! The only way you come at it is through mud or straight up a cliff face—and there was seven hundred Redcoats sitting on top of the rock looking down holding their bayonets on the ready."

"Aw, you're making it up," one of his companions said, red-faced. "They weren't looking down at us."

"How do you know? It was pitch dark. Anyway we step out, quiet and not talking, and wade through the marsh. Some of the boys are going up the river side. By this time their sentries know something is going on, and they're firing like crazy. And we keep coming. They don't seem to hit any of our boys—but then, we got bushes to hide behind. And inside of twenty minutes we're in the fort. And you know what them cowards are doing by then? Crying for mercy! 'Quarter, dear Americans, quarter!' they're screeching." He mimicked the terrified Redcoats with a satiric grin. "And General Wayne is right with us. Someone got him on the side of the head with a bullet, and he yells, 'Carry me up to the fort, boys!' and two of us helped him walk in, standing up. Whole thing didn't take more'n half an hour, and we did it with bayonets. Hardly fired a shot!"

"Is General Wayne going to be all right?"

"Oh, sure. It'd take more than a bullet crease alongside his skull to damage that one! He heard the boys yelling 'Fort's our own!' while he was walking in with us, and you'd a thought nothing ever touched him. He broke away and ran to join the cheering! Great officer!"

He looked beyond his audience and raised his nose like a bird dog scenting game. "Lads, I smell a tavern round the next bend in the road. On to the attack!"

They were in the Neutral Ground now. But no raiders were going to bother these men. They began marching faster and singing *Yankee Doodle* in quickstep time. Jock dropped out of the line and turned back toward home.

The triumph of Stony Point was so great it took awhile to sink in. The Patriots held King's Ferry again: a crucial spot in the control of the river. West Point, the important key fortress on the Hudson, was safe again.

Jock marched back to the forge, humming *Yankee Doodle* all the way.

Chapter 5

A MONTH after General Wayne's victory at Stony
Point, the neighbors in the Hudson Valley heard
that Major Henry Lee had taken Paulus Hook, with one
hundred and fifty-eight British prisoners. The Tories in
the valley became fearful and melancholy. The Patriots
began to hope the war would be soon won.

After those two American victories times were quiet
again, almost as quiet as before the war. But Maggie
Fraser complained that prices were going up faster than
she could ever remember. Sugar in the village store had
risen to five dollars a pound, and she didn't buy any. Her
family would have to get along on the honey from their
own bees. And coffee was almost as high.

"Perhaps we'll have to drink Liberty Tea after all," she
said, making a face at the thought. "At least we have the
strawberry and currant leaves in our own garden. And
then there's always sage."

Jock disliked all the Patriot tea substitutes, and he
didn't listen to his mother's plans.

"Mrs. Brady told me Hyperion tea from raspberry leaves
is most excellent," Maggie Fraser went on, just as if her

family were listening. "And goodness knows we've got all the raspberry bushes we need."

"Anything we don't have to pay for would be a good thing," her husband said. "The way prices are going up, by the time we've had dinner we can't pay the rent." He scowled. "You know what Fleming paid me for the musket he bought yesterday? Eight hundred dollars in paper. Somebody's crazy. Guns can't be worth eight hundred dollars. Must be the paper isn't worth anything at all."

"We'll stop buying coffee," Maggie Fraser decided. "But we can't get along without salt, and that's going up too. Maybe if they'll pay eight hundred dollars for muskets, they'll pay a thousand."

Her husband looked at her in exasperation. "If they paid ten thousand it wouldn't be enough, pretty soon. Might as well pick it out of the scrap basket and cut it into dollars, for all the Continental currency is going to be worth in another year." He considered the financial outlook for a moment. "So long as Cartwright will sell the gun barrels for paper, we can stay even."

But when the ironmaster's foreman stopped, on his way home from a New York delivery, and George Fraser ordered another load of gun barrels, the man shook his head. "Ain't got no more gun barrels."

"What do you mean, no more gun barrels? What's the matter up there on the plantation? Ore run out? You can't tell me Cartwright isn't making iron."

"No, sir!" The foreman nodded vigorously. "He's making iron all right. But he ain't selling it for paper no more. British pay silver."

George Fraser stared at him, and then far beyond him at the quiet river. "So that's how it's going to be. Well—tell him I'll find it somewhere else."

The foreman drove on. George Fraser watched him go, his eyes narrowed in thought. Jock cried, "No iron! What'll we do, Pa?"

His father shrugged. "I guess we'll do nothing for awhile, 'cept repair work."

Jock stood in the middle of the floor and looked around the forge. The rifling bench, with its tool, the screw of which twisted to cut a spiral inside the barrel, was against the wall. The crankwheel for fine-boring stood still. A pile of rough-hewn maple and walnut gunstocks lay piled in a corner. A finished musket stood in the corner, and two gunlocks lay on the work table.

"First thing tomorrow I'll ride up to Sterling's and see if I can get iron from him. You can take the rent money up to Cartwright. It's due then, and you see if you can talk him into lowering his price or taking paper for those gun barrels. Where does he think the rent money is coming from?"

September first was a cool, brisk, shining day, and Jock set out on the old mare, Ginger, pleased to be sent on an errand on such a day. The huge maples overhanging the road were beginning to turn scarlet. The housewives in the village were taking in sun-dried wash from the lines and bushes. About forty families lived in the little village two miles up the Croton from Fraser Forge, and all the men worked for the ironmaster.

The road led around the white-steepled church, beyond the little schoolhouse where Jock had learned his letters, and turned into a broad avenue shaded by linden trees leading up to the ironmaster's mansion on top of the hill. This was a spacious brick building with white pillars outlining a wide veranda across the front. Jock rode around to the back, fastened the mare at the hitching post, and knocked at the back door.

When he asked for Mr. Cartwright, the house-servant who opened the door led him through a richly carpeted hallway to a small waiting room. This was a rich man's house, and Jock stared at the rooms they passed with intense interest. He saw that the ceilings were high, white, and decorated with carving. The rugs were thick and soft, beautifully figured in rich colors. The chairs were upholstered in silks and velvets.

While he waited for the servant to call his master, Jock heard a chatter of women's voices, and Mrs. Cartwright swept down the broad stairway, silken skirts rustling, and a curling feather sweeping around her cheek from a saucy hat. Her three daughters followed demurely, as silken and delicate as their mother. They never had their arms in soapsuds to their elbows like Peggy, scrubbing on sheets, Jock thought. The footman held open the front door for them, and outside Jock could see the elegant carriage that had been ordered from England, with a handsome pair of bay horses.

When the door closed behind them, the house became quiet. Jock looked curiously around the room he was waiting in. On the wall above the fireplace was a full-length portrait of one of the daughters, in a golden gown, with a curl laid upon one shoulder that looked as if it would curl about his finger if he touched it. She seemed to be smiling at him, and he responded instinctively, reaching out to the portrait. Just then he heard a footstep and spun about, embarrassed to have been caught touching anything in this house.

"Jock Fraser?"

Mr. Cartwright looked very much the way Jock remembered him from years ago, wearing a red velvet coat with gold lace and gold buttons. Somehow Jock always seemed to think of Mr. Cartwright as wearing red velvet.

"Yes sir. I'm Jock Fraser."

The ironmaster sat heavily down on one of the fragile chairs and looked up at Jock.

"You've grown a lot," he said, sounding surprised. "Grown into a fine lad." He squinted at him. "What did you wish to see me about?"

"My father sends the rent money." Jock handed it to Mr. Cartwright, who waved it aside indifferently. "You can take it to my rent collector," he said. "He keeps my books."

On the wall above the fireplace was a full-length portrait

"Pa wants me to talk to you about gun barrels, sir."

"What about gun barrels? Why doesn't he talk to me himself? Is he sending a boy to do the work of a man?"

Cartwright's tone was complaining, but Jock had the feeling he hardly meant it that way; it was just a habit.

"He had to ride out to look for iron, sir."

The ironmaster looked at the boy sharply. "Trying to buy from someone else, hey?"

"He has to have iron to stay in business, sir."

"Hm." The master settled himself back in his chair, handling himself gently. "So. How many blanks did he want?"

"He has a contract for twenty guns a week, sir. We could use two or three dozen blanks at a time. Or more."

The master hitched himself forward and leaned both hands on the head of his cane.

"My driver stopped for Fraser's order, and your father sent him back without an order."

"Yes, sir. He thought there must be some mistake. But your man said you weren't selling for paper."

"No mistake," Cartwright said. Then, "The British will pay silver. Can you think of any reason why I should sell to Fraser Forge for paper?"

"No, sir." Jock was beginning to feel frightened.

"I'm loyal to my king," Cartwright said. "This rabble that keeps fighting him—destroying the countryside, depressing the currency . . . Well?" His voice sharpened demandingly.

"But he can't get silver these days," Jock said. He was dismayed to find himself sounding apologetic.

Cartwright pounded on the rug with his cane and raised his voice. "If he can't pay my prices, I can't afford to let him have any iron. Just tell him that, will you?"

"Yes, sir." Jock was angry, but he held it down and tried to sound reasonable. "Where will we get the money for the rent?"

Cartwright smiled, as if at last he had got the boy where he wanted him, and settled back in the chair, overflowing it at the edges.

"You've been making guns with your father? Apprentice?"

Jock said "Yes, sir," warily.

"I started out with my own father when I was your age, and worked at the furnace for years," Cartwright said, as if he were proud to remember those early days. "So I've got money now. Because I earned every penny of it." This was hardly true, Jock wanted to cry out, because most of his money came from his tenants. But it pleased Cartwright to represent himself as a self-made man, and the boy held his tongue. The man continued, sounding sorry for himself. "And who's going to keep all this business going when I'm gone? Look: you come and work for me, and you'll be rich some day. There's more money in iron than in gunsmithing. I never had a son . . ." He paused, letting his words weight down the silence.

"Thank you, sir. I'll—I'll think about it."

The promise of riches swirled through his mind, and, oddly, he remembered a gold watch. . . . His father had always said that in America a man could go as far as he wanted to go . . . perhaps this was the door opening for his father's son?

The ironmaster was struggling to his feet, and the boy held out a hand to help him.

"You think about what I said." Oliver Cartwright turned toward the door, leaning on his cane. "You could help your family." He stopped and looked at Jock, drawing together the heavy white brows. "If you were here with me, your father could have all the gun barrels he wants at his own price . . . and we wouldn't worry too much about the rent . . ."

Chapter 6

Jock thought about Mr. Cartwright's offer all the way back to Teller's Point. His mind toyed with all the possibilities. Skipping lightly over the next ten years or so, he dreamed of being a wealthy man in a velvet coat— only his would be blue, he thought. He'd drive around the valley in a rich carriage from England . . . but I'd have matched grays, he told himself. Or even white horses. Bays are so common.

He looked at his thin brown hands on the reins, hardened and callused from working at the forge, and tried to imagine them white and smooth. Illusions of grandeur danced before him. He would still be a Patriot. Perhaps, with all that money, he could be one of the Patriot leaders. He was vague about how the money would make him into one of the leaders of his country, but it seemed to him that if you had enough money you should be able to achieve anything you wanted with it.

He began planning how to tell his father about this great opportunity, and suddenly he came down to earth again, feeling as if he had hit it with a jolting thud. Pa wasn't going to like it.

George Fraser came back from the Sterling Iron Works

two hours after Jock returned. He could get no iron from Sterling, and anyway it wasn't right for gun barrels. That was the real trouble: in all the time the Frasers had lived in the Hudson Valley, the gunsmith had never heard of any furnace turning out iron as good for gun barrels as Cartwright's.

It seemed like a good time to explain Cartwright's offer.

"He said that, hah!" His Pa's eyes were blazing with quick rage. "I wouldn't let you work with that man if he had the last iron furnace in the entire country. He's no better than a common thief. He's just having trouble getting any boys to work for him. He's got more in mind than leaving his furnace to you, and don't you ever think different."

Feeling foolish, Jock went out to rub down the stocks for the last two guns in the shop. His father was right, of course. He should have known . . . And yet from time to time, his thoughts drifted again to wealth and riches, to being a gentleman . . . to money.

Major André and his gold watch. Since he had seen it, that gold watch seemed to have infected Jock's imagination. If you were rich, you could have a gold watch. You could command attention, admiration, public acclaim. Look how everyone watched when Mr. Cartwright went down the road to New York in his big, gaudy carriage.

Once, incautiously, he said that in his father's hearing.

Pa grunted scornfully. "Him with his fancy house and slaves and carriages and ladies in silks and satins! . . . And what has he got? A spineless kind of character trembling all the time in the winds of revolution. Afraid the colonies will win, afraid the Skinners will take some of his precious money some time, afraid of his shadow! That's what his money does for him!"

Jock didn't believe a word of it. And the thought of being a favorite of Mr. Cartwright's (wasn't that what the ironmaster had hinted at? He had said right out: "I never had a son") opened up a dream that glittered with all the colors of the rainbow.

Meantime he had to drudge along at the forge, mending old guns, because there was no iron for new ones, a dreary and unrewarding effort.

"It's a miracle if the Americans can win any war with guns like these," George Fraser said with profound contempt. "Look: crooked barrels, bad boring . . ." He held an old musket to the light, put a bowstring in the bore, and peered through it. "Those European smiths know better than this! They threw these guns together fast as possible, just to get American money. They're a disgrace to their makers."

It would have been so easy for Pa to get the iron for the new guns, Jock thought. Sometimes it seemed as if he would never understand Pa's stubborn pride.

Jock cut wood for fires, harvested apples, mended barn

and fence against the winter, as fall came down the valley. The maples burned scarlet, and the oaks turned gold. His mother and sister boiled up the soft soap they made at the end of fall butchering each year. Strings of apples and onions hung drying in the loft, and jars of pickles lined the shelves. But sugar was too high for jams this winter. Maggie Fraser was drying the fruit instead.

There wasn't much to do in the forge now. Occasionally guns came in for mending. Most guns had to be freshened and repaired now and then. But the repair business was not enough to make up for the loss of the army contract. The army had been paying well for Fraser muskets, and without that business there was little money coming in. Prices were going up faster than ever, and the next rent day came before Christmas.

Maggie Fraser said she could earn a little money running a hostelry, and Jock made a sign that said "Lodging for travelers" and hung it beside the rifle sign on the river road.

But there were not many travelers going past the Fraser house these days. The road ran through the Neutral Ground, and any traveler risked his money, if not his life, traveling that road, even in daylight.

The valley was full of soldiers coming and going. Mostly they were Americans who drifted down from West Point when they were on leave. Some of them stopped at the Frasers for a good meal on their way home. Some of them stayed the night. All of them were dirty, hungry, ragged, and glad to have their clothes washed and mended. But Maggie Fraser could not ask these soldiers for money. She felt they had earned a night's lodging, and she always asked about Rob. None of them had known her son. He had been gone six months now and his mother fretted about him.

"When I see these poor hungry boys I wonder how he's getting along," she said more than once. "Nobody even knows where he is. What if he's been taken prisoner and is in one of those dreadful British prisons somewhere? Wouldn't you think he'd at least write a letter?"

And then late in November the peddler came through. He carried dress materials for the ladies, and needles, pins and thread, and he came around to call on his customers about once a year, always bringing with him tales of the world outside the Hudson Valley. When he came this time the frost had settled into the ground, the bright leaves had fallen, and snow was spinning in the air. Jock was splitting wood, and he told the peddler to go right into the kitchen. And then he struck his axe into a log and followed him in.

He was about six feet six inches tall, the tallest man Jock had ever seen, as thin as a scarecrow, ragged and bent. He had looked, to Jock's eyes, about eighty years old as far back as the boy could remember. And yet he was spry and untiring.

Jock was splitting wood, and he told the peddler to go in

"Jeremiah Bolter!" Maggie Fraser welcomed him. "Come in and sit by the fire. There's a kettle of soup on the fire this minute."

"Don't mind if I do, Miz Fraser." He leaned over a little and let his pack slip to the floor; then he straightened up with a sigh of pleasure. "It's gettin' right cold out," he said, huddling close to the hearth. Mrs. Fraser filled a huge bowl with thick soup and set it before him.

"You're late coming around this season," she said.

"It ain't so easy to git around these days, what with the Skinners and Cowboys in that Neutral Ground, there," he said, and he leered at her with a bright blue eye. "Almost decided not to come this way till spring. But then I got a letter for the Frasers, down there in New Jersey, and I tell myself they're my friends, they'll want this letter. So I crossed over the river at Dobbs Ferry and come by Kakiat. Took about four days to find someone would row me across Slaughter's Landing. But I made it . . ." He was slapping his pockets, which hung around his coat like so many small sacks. "Now where could I have put that letter?"

"Who sent the letter, Jeremiah?" Maggie Fraser sounded eager.

"You'll be glad for this one," he promised. "Oh, here it is! Put it in my hat so's I'd be sure to remember it, and then nearly forgot!" He cackled as if that were the funniest joke he'd ever made, pulled the letter from the greasy band inside his hat, and handed it to Maggie, crumpled and dirty.

"Rob!" she shrieked. "Peggy! Jock! Rob sent us a letter! Where's Pa? Get him quick!"

Peggy jumped up and dropped her sewing. Jock ran out to the forge where his Pa was sharpening tools. Then they were all sitting around the trestle table, and George Fraser took the letter to read aloud.

> Dear Pa and Ma:
>
> It's been a long time since I hev heerd anything about folks in the valley, and I hope yew are all rite up there. I am with the army, and we hev been very busy marching back and forth. We air now in New Jersey where we will stay the winter. I can hire out to a farmer and maybe ern some money. His food will be better than the army wich has none. I hope I can come home in the spring. I miss yew all. But Gen'l Washington needs every man, and we air going to win this war.
>
> Yr Affekshunat son, Rob

Maggie was wiping her eyes and quietly sniffling. George Fraser read the whole letter through again to himself, looking pleased.

"He sounds all right," said Peggy, as if she wondered what her parents were so excited about.

Jock turned to Jeremiah, who was eating the thick hot soup in great gulps, at the same time trying to look as if he were somewhere else. "Where did you see Rob?" Jock asked. "How does he look?"

"I was acomin' through Morristown when I see him walkin' along the road," Jeremiah said. "He knew me—but then, I'm easy to find." He cackled loudly. "So he said, would I jist wait a minute while he writ a letter for me to take, and I said why sure, nothing to hurry me on."

"When was this?" Maggie asked suddenly.

"Oh, mebbe three, four weeks ago. I been walkin' since. But it's kinda slow these days."

Maggie was counting on her fingers. Six months till spring, when Rob said he might come home.

"Now I got some pretty stuffs I thought the ladies might like," Jeremiah said, opening his pack while the atmosphere was so soft and friendly.

Peggy loved a pretty fine brown woollen cloth with the cherry colored ribbons he laid upon it. Maggie Fraser fondled a shawl that had come from the continent, soft and fine and warm. And George Fraser sat scowling as his womenfolk gloated over the peddler's wares.

At last Maggie asked timidly, "How much do these things cost—now?"

"Too much," Jeremiah said with a wry grin. "Six hundred and fifty dollars paper. They'll be a thousand dollars by the time I come back this way in the spring. Paper is falling that fast . . ."

Maggie Fraser wrung her hands. "But we haven't got all that money, Jeremiah. Oh, I feel so bad about it. Here you brought Rob's letter and everything . . . Where will you go next?"

"Don't you fret your pretty head about me, Miz Fraser. I'll stop at North Castle for the winter. Got a friend there. The goods will keep . . ."

He began to fold up the cloth with care. George Fraser said, "I've got a piece of silver, Jeremiah. It isn't much. But it's worth more than paper. How about a silver crown?"

"Mr. Fraser, that will buy these things and a couple of ribbons thrown in!"

"Well—I guess we'd pay it just to hear from Rob. And if the women get a couple of pretties along with the letter it's more than worth it . . ." He pulled Major André's silver crown out of his pocket and handed it to the peddler. "And suppose you stay the night and start on to North Castle tomorrow."

"Thank ye, thank ye."

Peggy and her mother picked up their fabrics with bright eyes. Jeremiah bit the silver, spun it in the air, and put it in his worn leather wallet.

The next morning he was on his way with a letter for Rob from his family, in case he should run into someone who might be going down Morristown way in New Jersey, before spring.

The week after Jeremiah left the forge, the winter of 1779 set in with a violent blizzard and temperatures that froze the Croton River for the first time in twenty years.

Chapter 7

GEORGE Fraser was irritable all the time these days. Nothing Jock could do was right, and the boy was angry in his turn. When he looked about the forge, empty of iron or work, save for half a dozen old guns awaiting repair, it looked like a rag-picking business. And when he picked up one of the broken guns that had come from Europe for the Colonial army, he threw it down in disgust. A fine gunsmith shouldn't even bother with these pieces of junk. No wonder Pa was angry as a wounded bear all the time. But still . . .

"Don't take on so," his mother told him once, when he was complaining, "your pa is worried sick about the rent. It's the first time in his life he hasn't paid it on the day."

Rent day had passed, and Jock had forgotten. "But what will he do if there's no money?"

His mother was worried and sad. "I don't know, I'm sure. Your pa has slaved all these years, a fine craftsman, making fine guns, and never been in debt in his life. It eats at a man not to be able to earn a living."

But it might have been easy for Pa, if he had let Jock go to work for the ironmaster. The boy let himself dream again: Pa working all the time at fine guns, finer than anything he had made yet. No worries about iron or rent money. And his wealthy son driving around in a carriage, bringing presents . . . Something about the dream wasn't quite right, and Jock shook his head. He couldn't tell what it was, except he knew Pa would likely cut his throat, if he signed indentures with Mr. Cartwright.

He went out to the forge again. "Pa? You want me to go up to the big house and tell them we aren't paying any rent this quarter?"

George Fraser looked stooped as he moved among the tools that hung unused in the smithy. But he straightened up at Jock's question and glared at him.

"You're never to go near that man, you hear?" His voice was trembling with anger. "He has no right to take a man's livelihood from him. He'll pay for it some day."

Jock shook his head over Pa's stubbornness. Another rent day was coming up in March. Every three months they owed more money. And there was none these days, not even paper. They were mending the army guns for credit. Even the army had no money.

The worst winter in memory closed in. The highlands along the Hudson were covered with snow, black storm clouds lowered over the valley day after day, and disappeared only when the snow fell so heavily, or the wind blew it so violently that none could see more than a yard before him.

The roads were blocked waist-high with snow, and bitter winds howled down the river, day after day. No traveler ventured along the roads, and for four months the world outside of Fraser's forge seemed to sleep through the winter.

But even the worst of winters blows itself out when the world has turned enough to bring the spring. The early days of March went by, the waters were running high, the snow was still blowing out of the north whenever spring approached too closely.

April came on, the snow melted, the streams filled with freshets, buttercups and violets suddenly blossomed, the trees began to swell with leafbuds. The roads opened up and people moved cautiously back and forth. Mrs. Fraser had a guest for the night now and then. The winter was behind them, and another year of war was about to begin.

And the first week in April the rent collector came to call.

"How does he expect me to find money when there's no iron to work with?" George Fraser snarled. "Get out of here! And don't come back again!" He grabbed his rifle and pointed it at the rent collector, who backed out the door and stood there, trying to look scornful.

"Now, now, there's no need to get all upset," he admonished the gunsmith. "Mr. Cartwright is not unreasonable. We won't say any more about the rent just now. With summer coming on, things will improve. I just wanted to find out how things were going."

He stepped back farther, untied his horse, and mounted. Then as he moved out of rifle range, he called back, "By September you better have the money. The landlord can't let back rents go too long or he'd never collect!"

Fraser lowered the rifle, trembling with rage, and passed his hand across his brow. He set the gun down and stood in the door, looking broodingly at the great river and the towering hills.

Before September, Jock thought. How could they earn the money before September for a whole year's rent, when nothing had changed since last September? There was no silver, and the paper currency kept going down. Paper was printed in dollars now, instead of in British pounds. But it didn't make the money any better. The dollars dropped even faster than the pounds.

If they had been farmers instead of craftsmen, Jock thought gloomily, they could be selling what they grew for the same high prices they had to pay, and they'd have some money . . . He shook his head. He knew what happened to tenants who didn't pay their rent. He knew of the old man whose crops had failed last year: he'd been taken into court before the landlord's own judge, and sentenced to flogging and imprisonment. He was torn again, between wishing to run right off to Cartwright and sign the papers that would save his father from a debtor's prison, and knowing that Pa would feel worse about that than about his own troubles. If the colonies could just win this war that had been going on for five years now, he thought, a lot of problems would disappear—if they could wait that long!

He went to the store in the village one day late in May, to barter some maple sugar, some fresh-laid eggs, and one of their hams for a hundredweight of flour. The roadsides were flowering in the sun, the apples were forming on the trees, the wind was soft, and the river warm and lazy. Surely there was no place quite so lovely as their own Hudson Valley, Jock thought, as he rode along. Surely they would not have to leave this pleasant place.

The village was buzzing with news: Lafayette had returned from France on May tenth, and the French were sending men and ships to help the Americans! Jock thought immediately of what this could mean to his father, and quick optimism bubbled again. With the French armies, maybe the war would be over by the end of the summer. Maybe when the war was over, the landlord could collect no more rent. He could not reason out why this should be so, except that the landlord was a Tory, and if the Colonials won, the Tories might have to leave. It seemed as if victory ought to mean this for the Frasers.

As he approached the Croton River Bridge, the quiet air was shattered with threatening voices and gunfire, yells, oaths, and more gunfire, across the bridge. Jock pulled his horse off the road behind a clump of trees and waited. The gunfire was repeated three, four, five times

. . . It was the same gun, and Jock had never heard of a gun that could be fired in such quick succession.

On the other side of the river a boy ran toward the bridge, carrying a rifle and watching over his shoulder for pursuers. Two ruffians were chasing him. He paused, aimed his rifle, and fired. One of his pursuers fell in the road clutching his leg, and cursing; the other stopped beside his fallen comrade, shaking his fist and yelling after the boy who ran with pounding steps across the Croton Bridge and into the trees near Jock. There he stopped, sagging against the trunk of a giant maple, panting with deep breaths.

Jock watched him cautiously. You had to be careful these days whom you spoke to, and this boy had a rifle against which Jock's own rifle would be useless. He appeared to be a couple of years older than Jock.

The boy took another deep breath and stood up straight, looked about warily, and began to walk through the trees toward Jock. His thin face was brown and determined, his eyes were gray and hard, and when he saw Jock he raised the rifle to his shoulder in a quick reflex.

"I'm not going to shoot!" Jock cried. "Who are you?"

"What are you doing there?" the boy demanded suspiciously, his rifle unwavering.

"I'm riding home, over to Teller's Point. Where are you from?"

"I just want to be let alone. I had a little trouble, t'other side of the river, and I'm not looking for more."

"You musta fallen in with Skinners. I don't want to fight."

The boy approached slowly. Then, satisfied that Jock was not about to attack him, he lowered the gun.

"I heard tell about the Skinners back there at Tarrytown," he said. "I didn't plan to meet up with them."

"You came up from Tarrytown?"

The boy nodded. "I sure did. I'm dead tired of this war. All I want is out."

Jock looked at the boy's clothes: nondescript and dirty, they looked like something he might have worn on a farm. Yet he spoke of getting out of the war.

"Where were you fighting?" Jock asked.

"I was in the British army," the boy said, a little sullenly. Then, proudly, "I fought at Brandywine. We won that one, but what difference did it make? I been marching back and forth in this wild country, sitting around Philadelphia the winter after Brandywine, sitting around New York this winter. We don't seem to be getting on with it, and I'm sure sick of the army."

"How old are you?"

"Eighteen. I was only fifteen when I was at Brandywine."

"How'd you get into the army so young?"

"I was apprenticed to a gunsmith back in London, and I couldn't take the master any more. He was vicious, that he was. The best place to run away and hide was the army. They took anyone wanted to go to the colonies.

65

But it's no better than being an apprentice. They don't need me any more. I just decided to get out and now I gotta find some work."

"My pa's the best gunsmith this part of the country," Jock cried. "He's been wanting an apprentice . . . but there's no iron," he remembered, crestfallen.

The boy looked calculating. "There'll be iron some day," he said. Then for the first time he grinned. "My name's Dick Conway. I been wandering this part of the country four days now, and those Skinners back there were the first people I seen in all that time."

"The Neutral Ground is bad country. You want to come home with me? Ma will give you something to eat."

"Don't mind if I do. I haven't eaten anything for three days 'cept some honey I found in an old tree, and a dried loaf of bread in an empty house back there . . ."

Jock looked at his gun: a rifle, shorter than the long rifle Jock knew, and beautifully designed. "What kind of gun is that? I never heard a gun fire so fast."

Dick showed it to him. "It's a Ferguson. Ever heard of them?"

"Never did. I've handled a long rifle. But how does it fire so fast?"

"It loads like this." Dick gave the trigger guard a full turn, loaded the gun on the top of the breech, raised it to his shoulder, and fired at a rabbit hopping along the road a hundred yards ahead. The rabbit dropped.

"Lemme see that again!" Jock set down his own rifle,

Jock examined the Ferguson

and examined the Ferguson. A full turn of the trigger guard made an opening on top of the breech. When the ball was dropped into the opening it ran into the barrel far enough to let powder be poured in behind it. The opening closed with another full turn of the trigger guard. It could be loaded and discharged faster and more dependably than any other gun Jock had ever seen.

"Can I try it?"

Dick gave him a rifle ball. Jock turned the trigger guard, dropped in the ball and powder, closed the opening, raised the gun and fired.

"My sakes!" he breathed. "There's never been a gun like that! Where'd it come from?"

"Colonel Patrick Ferguson invented it back in England. He was my commanding officer at Brandywine, and we used some of his rifles there."

"Why doesn't the whole British army have them?"

Dick shrugged. "Who knows? I heard there were only two hundred made and issued before Brandywine. I guess there haven't been any since. Anyway, I got one of them. And when I left the army, I figured I'd earned the gun."

"Could you make this gun yourself?"

"I daresay. I was working for the gunsmith that made the first rifles for Colonel Ferguson. He wouldn't let me do very much. But I saw how he did it, and I could take this one apart and figure out the rest of it."

"Come along," Jock said. "I want Pa to see that gun."

Chapter 8

GEORGE Fraser took Dick in as an apprentice in spite of the lack of work. A good apprentice was hard to find, even in the best of times. And Fraser knew after one day in the forge that Dick Conway was well trained, skilled, and talented. Without iron to work with, and with no more work than Fraser could handle alone, the new boy was another mouth to feed. But the Ferguson rifle was a powerful attraction. The gunsmith, like his son, wanted to make a gun like it, and could not bear to let this one go elsewhere.

He examined the gun carefully, the day the boy arrived. "Nothing I'd like better than to make a gun like that! Hide it away, and don't let anyone see it or even know you have it." He handed it back to Dick with rough exasperation. "All we can do around here is fix the terrible pieces that came over from those thieving Continental gunsmiths." It hurt him like a physical pain to work with such poor products.

However, Dick didn't seem to mind the poorly made guns as much as George Fraser did. Once he said, with a half-smile, "There's nothing like a tour of duty in the army to make you appreciate a nice, quiet, well-fed apprenticeship—even working on only these junk pieces."

He was a good workman, the first apprentice Fraser had ever had, even including his own sons, who worked well enough to please the gunsmith, and Fraser told Dick that he'd qualify for a journeyman as soon as they had enough iron for him to make a whole gun.

Jock, listening, knew what the careful praise meant: Pa had never believed any apprentice was really a good workman before. He'd never told Jock he would make a fine gunsmith, and the boy glowered in uneasy jealousy. Some days he guessed Pa wouldn't care if he was there or not. And he comforted himself with dreams of working for Cartwright and turning out to be a greater gunsmith than the colonies had ever seen . . . .

The week after Dick moved in, the Cowboys crossed the Croton and raided Green's farm, two miles away. They stole his four cows and two horses. The call went out for a meeting at Mead's Tavern at Crompond. Jock went with his father, and Dick stayed home with the womenfolk. He didn't want to be seen in public.

An angry farmer cried, "Any one of us could be next! We've got to protect ourselves! Nobody else will . . ."

"Where were the militia?" someone demanded. "They're supposed to be protecting us north of the Croton."

The blacksmith from the village looked cynical. "Some folks wouldn't be surprised if Cartwright hired the Cowboys hisself, to keep his tenants in line."

One of the farmers stood up and pounded on the table. "How long do we have to pay these rents to that bloodsucker?" he shouted. "Why can't we buy our little piece of ground and leave it to our children? Cartwright has a hundred thousand acres! And there's nothing left for anyone that wants a little ground for hisself!"

"Farmers struck about the rents, years ago," someone recalled.

"Yes, and what good did it do? I tell you, men, the only way we'll get out from under the landlords is to win this war! If General Washington wins this valley, you'll see old Cartwright running away fast enough!"

Someone else said, "We're fighting for independence, ain't we? How can a man be independent, if he's forever tied to a landlord?"

"Old Cartwright has got his own company of guards," Farmer Green announced. "Why doesn't he look after his tenants so the Cowboys don't steal our stock?"

There was bitter laughter. The tenants all owed Cartwright rent money and allegiance. But he owed them nothing. At least, Jock thought, listening to the angry debate, his father was not the only one behind in his rent.

He thought about the meeting all the way home. Nothing had been settled, except that each man must look out for himself, because there were not enough militiamen to protect the valley.

If there weren't enough militia, Jock thought, they needed him. Now that Dick had moved in, even Pa couldn't fuss about being short-handed in the forge without Jock.

The next day he rode to North Castle and joined up.

"Regular or volunteer?" the man at the desk asked him, pulling out the muster book.

"Volunteer." The volunteer militia worked with the Skinners who were mostly Patriots, against the Cowboys, who were mostly Loyalist.

The man wrote his name down. "Can you find your own gun and shot?"

"Yes, sir."

"Now you're on the muster roll of the New York State Volunteer Militia. Any time the call comes from the Continental army, you have to answer for regular duty. Meantime, you'll be on sentry-watch every other night. Captain Cooper will give you the schedule. Ride down to his house and get it. Keep your gun and ammunition ready, and bring along as much food as you'll need for the night."

"Yes, sir."

He hadn't realized till that minute that he'd have to get clothes ready. There was no special uniform for the militia—it was hard enough to find uniforms for the regular army.

When Jock mounted, a couple of armed men followed him down the road. A mile from North Castle they pulled up and told him to stop.

"What's your name, son?" drawled one of them, a dirty

man with a tangled beard. The other was a surly-looking red-bearded man, equally dirty. "What militia you in?"

"Jock Fraser. Volunteer militia."

"Well, Jock, we can use you. Us Skinners are going out tonight and look for the Cowboys that raided Green's farm t'other night. Might as well go along and learn how we operate."

"What about getting my schedule from Captain Cooper?"

"Haw! You got it, son!" said the red-bearded man. "This here is Captain Cooper!"

Jock's hand flew to his head in salute, and Captain Cooper smiled sourly. "We don't bother much with military stuff. All we want to do is catch the Cowboys."

"Yes, sir. Where do I meet the Skinners?"

"Docker's farm at sundown. You know where that is?"

"Down Tarrytown Road near the little Dutch church?"

"Right enough."

"If I can get away," Jock muttered, not so eager as he had been at the tavern last night.

The dark-bearded captain scowled ferociously. "If you ain't there, we'll come and get you. When you enlist in the Skinners, you ain't playing games."

Jock rode home thinking hard. He was going to be sixteen before Christmas, and Dick Conway had fought at Brandywine when he was fifteen. He hadn't somehow expected the Skinners to be like this. But then he wondered why not. Everything he had ever heard about them sounded like the men he had met. His blood began to rise with excitement. The people in the Hudson Valley needed protection, and now he was part of the protecting force.

He rode into the stableyard with his head high. He was in the army now, and if Pa and Ma were going to stop him, he'd have to run away. That was simple enough.

"Where you been all this day?" George Fraser demanded, as Jock turned the horse loose.

"Joining up." Jock's heart began to pound heavily.

"You—what?!"

"I enlisted in the volunteer militia, Pa."

His father was silent for several minutes. Then, "Volunteer militia, huh? That's the gang of cut-throats call themselves the Skinners?"

"I guess it's the same, Pa. After I heerd about Mr. Green's raid last night, I figured somebody has to help fight the Tories."

Another silence. Then, "Your gun ready?"

"Yes, sir. All I need is powder and bullets."

"We'll make a supply. When do you get called out?"

"Tonight, at sunset. Docker's farm. They're going after the Cowboys, and get Mr. Green's cattle back for him, I guess."

George Fraser looked suddenly older. "I hadn't counted on losing two boys to the army."

"I figured now you got Dick he's worth more to you than I am."

His pa looked at him keenly, and Jock colored. He knew his jealousy of Dick was childish. He wished he could get rid of the foolish feeling in words, but nothing seemed to come.

"Well . . ." Mr. Fraser found nothing more to say either. "Just keep out of the way of bullets. And don't get your ma upset."

They walked in to supper, and sat down at the trestle table each thinking his own thoughts. And then George Fraser said, "Well, I guess I'd rather have you with the Skinners, at that, than working for that old Tory up on the hill."

Maggie Fraser whipped around from the kettle, where she was spooning up dumplings and chicken stew. "Who's in the Skinners? Jock? You didn't!! George, why didn't you stop him?"

"Now, Maggie, he's getting to be a man pretty fast. And the volunteer militia isn't like the regular army. He'll be around home most of the time."

Maggie set her lips and put the food on the table, slamming dishes around the way she did when she was angry. Dick ate his stew with great relish, as if he didn't hear a word of the conversation.

"When I think of Rob being off somewhere, nobody knows where, probably not having enough to eat . . ." Maggie Fraser went on in a low sputtering tone, "Honestly! Sometimes I think it's hardly worthwhile to be a Patriot."

"It wouldn't do you any good to be a Tory," her husband reminded her.

"Oh, I know. But I get so sick of this war going on and on. Jock was only ten years old when it started—who ever thought it would go on long enough for him to fight?"

"Come now, Maggie. We live in a hard time. But it'll be past, some day."

"I don't believe it! I think the war will go on the rest of our lives—taking our children and throwing them away . . ."

She mopped her eyes with the corner of her apron, blew her nose, and looked sternly at Jock. "Whatever else you do, stay out of the way of the bullets," she told him. And then, as if she were comforting herself with small assurances, she said, "At least you can eat your meals at home. You won't have to go hungry."

So in the end his family took it better than he had expected, and Jock was almost disappointed. He'd been prepared to fight for the right to fight, if he had to, and here they were, giving in like this. It was kind of a let-down.

But after supper, with the sun reddening low in the west, when he got on Ginger, carrying his powder horn and a bag of bullets, and his rifle in his hand, a sense of adventure surged up: he was going out tonight with the Skinners. He was a soldier!

There were twenty men at the patrol meeting at Docker's farm, when Jock rode up. Captain Josh Cooper looked at him and checked off his name. "We're all here now. Whitey, you take your men and ride south along the Tarrytown road, and take some of the lanes in between. Rest of us are going down the White Plains road. Don't forget, anyone you can pick up, the gov'mint says we can keep anything we get. If it's a bunch of Cowboys, mebbe we can get ransom money."

The men divided into two roughly equal parties, and Captain Cooper called his patrol together once more, before they set off.

"If we find any Cowboys, we take them for prisoners, understand? No killing, if we can take them without."

Jock rode at the end of the patrol. They rode in pairs where the road was wide enough, and fell into single file where it narrowed. As they crossed a bridge and resumed riding in pairs, in the Neutral Ground, the man ahead of Jock was talking about the night before.

"Did you hear they caught Ethan and Jeb last night on the way back from Tarrytown?"

"Didn't kill 'em?"

"Naw. Cowboys talked about taking them to White Plains as prisoners, and then decided it was too much trouble. So they jist took horses and guns, and turned Ethan and Jeb loose to walk back again. Made the boys sore to lose the horses, though."

They were keeping their voices low, but the words drifted back to Jock. Then a warning went down the line: "Keep it quiet. Someone's ahead." The talking ceased.

Jock rode at the end of the patrol

Jock heard other hoofbeats, another party of riders, and his heart began to pound, partly from hope, partly from fear, that the other party would prove to be Cowboys. He balanced his rifle, feeling the powder horn and pouch of balls. It seemed as if he'd been waiting for this moment all of his life, yet it had come too soon and he was unprepared.

He thought of the Ferguson rifle. A man could practically win a war single-handed with that gun. He wished so hard that he had one right now, his mouth watered with longing. Mebbe the Skinners would raid old man Cartwright's place one night, mebbe he could pick up some gun barrels and take them home to work on.

There was a shout in the dark. "Who goes there?" He couldn't tell whether it was his own party, or the other party challenging. A musket sounded once, then another musket, and hoofbeats were fleeing.

"Well, boys, guess we got this road cleared," Cooper said. "We'll ride another couple of miles, and then go back."

One or two of the men near Jock left the patrol. He could hear them turning off at lanes that were almost invisible. The rest of the patrol rode back to the intersection with the Tarrytown road, sat there half an hour, then rode back along a little-used road that was narrow and dusty. Not another sound rose in the night.

Jock went home at dawn. He was disappointed that no pitched battle had been joined. On the other hand, they had cleared the road of someone who shouldn't be on it.

Chapter 9

O N a day in late July Jock tore into his mother's kitchen screaming "Rob's home! Ma! Rob's coming!" And then, before his mother could set down the milk pan and turn around, the boy was gone again, running up the muddy road, arms waving like wings, to meet his brother Rob, home from the war.

As he drew closer to the plodding figure, his pace slackened. Jock was suddenly shy before this brother who had been gone for more than a year.

Rob was slogging along, painfully tired, and he looked as if he could barely keep his musket on his shoulder. His face was grimy, with a week's growth of beard, his eyes looked out of black hollows. His clothes were filthy and tattered, and he was barefoot.

"Rob?" Jock asked, uncertainly.

The man smiled. And through the mud and beard and hollows of starvation, it was Rob's smile. Jock flung himself into his brother's arms and then, embarrassed, he pulled away again and fell into step beside him.

"I'll carry the gun," he offered. He reached out and took the musket on his own shoulder, and Rob walked more easily without it.

Jock wanted to ask, "How could you get so worn out? Don't they feed you in the army? Were you in prison?" But he held the questions back. Rob looked too tired to talk.

The July day was hot and fragrant. A three days' rain had freshened the fields, and though the roads were muddy, the red clover and Queen Anne's lace, the wild mustard and shaggy daisies along the roadside glowed under brilliant skies. Even Rob lifted his haggard face and sniffed the fragrance.

"Smells like home," he said.

"How far did you come?"

"Started early this morning. I guess it's about twenty miles today. I been sick a couple of weeks. That's why they let me have a furlough." He laughed with a little twisted sound that turned into a cough. "They know a man can get some good food if he goes home. The army's been living on scraps for a month now."

Something clutched at Jock's stomach, but it wasn't hunger. He felt as if he couldn't eat a thing, not ever again. Rob had been healthy and strong, gay and laughing, when Jock had seen him last, before he ran away to enlist. How could they send him home like this, hungry and exhausted, a wreck of the brave lad who had gone to fight?

"Ma has a pot of stew," Jock muttered, trying to say something comforting. "I guess you can have a good meal right away."

Ma was running down the road, arms flung wide

Maggie Fraser was running down the road, arms flung wide to welcome her homecoming son. "Rob! Rob! I thought you were never coming home again!"

"Aw, Ma, you don't want to touch me till I get some clean clothes on," he protested. But she clung to him anyway. "It's so good to have you home!"

Then, wiping her eyes and standing away from him, as he stared about the kitchen, looking almost too big for the little house, she declared, "It's shocking the way the army treats the men. I've got a big tub of warm water all ready for you . . . unless you want something to eat first?"

He shook his head. "I got a meal along the road, couple of hours ago. I'd rather get clean first."

He disappeared behind the curtain in the corner of the kitchen, where the big washtub was filled with steaming water, with a floating sponge and a cake of homemade soap smelling of bayberry, and Ma said to Jock, "You go and bring out your brother's clothes. My stars, I never saw anything like it! Take him these clean things to put on while I'm scrubbing that uniform."

Jock carried the lice-infested filthy clothes out to the tub at the back of the yard, where they could soak in strong soap and hot sun for awhile. He could stand going without food in the army, he told himself, feeling heroic. But he didn't think he could stand the bugs.

By the end of the day Rob was a different man from the one who had slogged up the muddy road a few hours ago. He was clean and shaven, his hair washed and brushed and neatly tied back. He wore the civilian clothes he had left behind: a blue coat and smallclothes, immaculate full-sleeved white shirt, white stockings, and buckled shoes. His eyes were not so hollow: he had already eaten a hearty meal of stew and dumplings and apple pie from the early-ripened yellow apples in the dooryard.

"It's a pity, truly, that you can't cook for the army, Ma," he said, sighing with appreciation. "If a man could eat like that every day, we'd have driven the British into the sea months ago."

Dick Conway was listening to Rob's tales of the past year.

"Armies are all alike," he said. "That's why I ducked out when I could."

Rob glanced at him with a measuring glance. There was some constraint between the Patriot fighter in the Fraser house and the British deserter.

"We Patriots always think it shows good sense when you leave the British and come over to us," he said with a little smile. "Of course, when a man is going the other way, he's a traitor."

But surely no American left the cause to turn to the enemy, Jock thought, shocked at the idea. Of course there was that strange Dr. Church, whose treachery was uncovered five years ago. But nobody else . . .

A small chill fell upon the company, as if Rob's words meant more than they said. Dick stiffened, leaned back where his face was in shadow, and said no more. But Dick never did talk much.

It was funny about Dick. He was a fine workman, polite, helpful. But he didn't open up. He answered questions, but said as little as possible. He wasn't really a cheerful kind of person, and Jock felt that he knew him no better now than when Dick had come home with him six weeks before.

The late-day summer sun was warm, the fresh wind blowing from the east smelled of the sea, and Rob stretched in lazy contentment.

"When you come home on leave, you sure find out what you're fighting for," he said. "I'll be glad when this war is won and the country is ours, and we can settle down to building again."

"How long will that be?" his mother asked. She sounded as if the answer were very important.

"Who knows?" He yawned deeply. "The French ships arrived in Newport a week ago—let's hope it will make a difference. We can hang on—maybe better than the Redcoats can. Some of them are pretty sick of the war." Dick looked away at the highlands across the river and he compressed his mouth.

"Plenty of us are tired of war," he said. "Lots of the boys, either they're homesick, or else they want to settle here. Either way, they're wondering what all the fighting is about."

George Fraser asked how the army was fixed now for

guns, and told Rob about the lack of iron for Fraser Forge.

"What about the quitrent, Pa?"

"Aye. What about it? It'll have to be owing, I guess, till the war's over and I can make a little money again." His father took his pipe out of his mouth and spoke intensely. "What this war means to me is getting rid of some of the leeches that hold all the land in the valley, and letting some of us common people have a chance to buy our own. I don't see any other way to open up this valley, or for me to get land. That's what I'm fighting for. If the British win, I might as well give up and leave the Hudson Valley. And here is where I want to stay." He thought about that a moment. Then he asked Rob, "When do you have to go back?"

"In a week. I'll be in the West Point garrison then."

"West Point, hey?" Pa looked up with lively interest. "I remember the British trying to take the Point back in 1777 before there was a fort there. Right before Saratoga, it was. They've never come so close to holding the Hudson since. General Washington had that Polish officer building the fort right after that. Did you know I helped forge the chain they hung there, across the river?"

"You mean when you were working up the river all winter, two years back?" Rob asked. "I never knew it was the chain. What's it like?"

"Oh, it's a good one. Links were like so—about two feet long." He gestured with both hands to show the size of the links of the chain. "Two and a quarter inch iron . . . but that was three years ago. Must be needing a little repair by now . . ."

"What was the chain for?" Jock wanted to know.

George Fraser was puffing on his pipe, looking relaxed as he talked war business with his older son. He was pleased with Jock's question.

"They supported the chain on logs, and those must be getting water-soaked by now. It kept ships from going up the river beyond the Point. When I saw it laid two years ago, it woulda stopped any ship. By now, I don't know . . . mebbe you garrison boys will be fixing it."

Rob nodded. "They say West Point is the most important fortification in this war," he said.

"That so? Most important fortification, you say? And right here in the Hudson Valley. H-m-m-m-" His father looked very pleased at this bit of news, and took his pipe out of his mouth and waved it at Rob. "I'd be proud to make more links for that chain, if they need any help," he said. It was evident that he took as much pride in that West Point chain as in any guns he had made. "Biggest chain I ever see."

"Our men heerd the General is reinforcing West Point. That means he's afraid Clinton is going to go for the Point. And if he took that fort the war would be over." Rob looked sober and yet excited about the prospect of defending this critical spot.

"Think you can hold it, Rob?"

"Oh, sure we can hold it. Till he blows us all out of it, that is." Rob spoke as if this was the surest thing about the war. "Our men are good at fighting. They aren't so good at sitting around hungry and dirty for weeks at a time, while the British take Carolina." He shook his head. "One step forward, two steps back. That's the way we seem to be running this war."

"Did Jock tell you he enlisted in the volunteer militia?" Jock could hear some pride in Pa's voice, and it made him feel good. Rob swiveled toward Jock.

"Is that right? The volunteer militia saved a supply train for General Washington more than one time. We like the militia—they're pretty important, when it's so hard to keep the men in the army."

Jock was swelling with satisfaction. Dick seemed to have withdrawn farther back into the shadows. "I go out with the militia every other night," Jock said. "So far nothing much has happened."

Rob laughed aloud. "That's the story of the whole army! March here, march there, stand around and wait. Something happens about once a year. Mebbe I've been lucky. At least no one shot at me yet. And I don't expect any action out of this West Point assignment, either."

George Fraser took his pipe out of his mouth and spoke profoundly.

"I gotta feeling you'll see action in West Point, son. No telling what kind. But something's going to happen up that way, mark my words."

Chapter 10

THE week after Rob rode away, his saddlebags loaded with food, his uniform clean, mended and spruce, an American officer rode up to the horse trough on a big black horse, watered the horse, and then rode around to the forge. Jock stopped work and saluted. He felt obliged to salute officers, even in his ragged work clothes, now that he belonged to the militia.

"Yes, sir," he said. "Can we help you, sir?"

The officer looked tall, sitting up on that big horse. But at Jock's greeting George Fraser came out of the workroom. The officer swung down, and stood beside the horse, holding its bridle.

He was rather short, only five feet seven or so, stocky and very muscular, with light eyes blazing in a sun-darkened face. As he moved toward George he limped noticeably on one leg.

"Mr. Fraser? General Arnold, at your service."

He held out his hand to shake the hand of the gunsmith, and he looked directly at Jock, smiling. Jock gulped. General Arnold! One of the greatest heroes in Washington's army was standing here in Fraser Forge, shaking his father's hand!

Benedict Arnold carried himself with a head-high pride that made him seem tall, and after his first fleeting impression Jock thought the General was a tall man.

"I've been told, sir, that you're the finest gunsmith in this part of the country. I expect to be commanding at West Point within the week, and I wanted to make your acquaintance. I know we'll need work on the guns there."

George Fraser, topping the General by two inches, met his eyes and nodded. He didn't smile at him. But George never smiled at anyone easily. He was a cautious man, and he liked to know what he thought of someone before he acted friendly with them.

"We can mend guns, General Arnold," he said, speaking as if he were just as good as the General, polite but perfectly sure of himself. "We're having a little trouble getting barrels for new ones. But we can still fix old ones."

"All we've got are old ones," the General said, looking satiric. "If you can fix those we'll need no others."

"Happens I worked on the chain up there at the Point," George Fraser said. "Have you looked at it lately?"

"That's most interesting," said the General. He spoke in a rather harsh voice, but his bright eyes showed intense interest in every comment George made. "I'll be checking the boom as soon as I take command."

Fraser nodded. "Just take a good look, General. Some of the joints will need fusing by this time."

The General turned to his horse. "On my way here,

my stirrup broke," he said. "I know this is not work for a craftsman like a gunsmith. But if you could mend it for me, I'd be most grateful."

"These days we take any work that comes along," George Fraser said. "If you'll just tie him up, right here, I'll mend it so it won't come apart again."

Jock tore himself away and ran to the house.

"Ma," he said in a tense whisper, "General Arnold is out there talking to Pa. Shouldn't we give him something to eat?"

"Sakes!" She looked out toward the forge. "General Arnold! Of course he'll be hungry. What's your pa thinking of, not to bring him to the house? You go and ask him will he take a bit of supper. Peggy! Make the table ready for the General to sit down."

Jock ran back to the forge. The General was still talking to Pa, who was examining the stirrup and pointing out the weakness where it had broken.

"Sir, my mother wishes you to stop and have supper with us. You must be hungry after such a ride."

General Arnold turned his sharp eyes to Jock and smiled.

"I'll be glad enough for something to eat, my lad. I've ridden forty miles today, and must go back to Kakiak before sundown to meet with General Washington."

"I guess to reach there you'd better ride up to King's Ferry to cross," George Fraser said.

"It looks like a lot more riding, any way I plan it,"

General Arnold said, in a light tone that suggested he wished to be a little more informal with these pleasant people.

The three walked back to the house. The General limped heavily, using a walking stick and trudging as if he were determined not to let a bad leg slow him down. Jock recalled the stories of his victories: he had gotten the leg wound first at Quebec, and again, a year later in the same leg at Freeman's Farm, when he had led the troops to that great victory that resulted in General Burgoyne's surrender with his whole army at Saratoga.

They sat down at the table, and Maggie set fresh-baked warm bread before the General, with a large pot of strawberry jam. She apologized because she had to make it with honey instead of sugar. But Jock didn't know why she was apologizing. It still tasted better than anybody else's jam. There was cold roast pork, some hard cooked eggs, and a bowl of warm applesauce. The General ate as if he were starved.

"I like to see a man enjoy his food," Maggie Fraser said, smiling at General Arnold so that her dimple showed. "It seems as if a great general ought to enjoy it even more than average."

"Any man would enjoy food like this more than average," General Arnold told her, holding her eyes as if he liked looking at her. "You know, when I bring my wife and child here soon, it will be comforting to know we are in the midst of friends."

Peggy, who had been watching him with shy alertness, spoke up suddenly. "Oh, I know about your wife!"

"You do?" General Arnold was surprised.

"Last summer Major André stopped here once. He showed me a sketch of another Peggy in Philadelphia, and then he said she had married one of our greatest generals. Why, General Arnold, I feel as if I knew her already!"

"So you know Major John André! A good friend of mine, even if, unfortunately, we're fighting on opposite sides in this war." He sighed, and then said, "When this sad conflict is ended I hope all our people can be united again in friendship."

"I just hope the conflict will be ended before my boy is killed," Maggie said a little grimly. "He tells us he'll be in the West Point garrison, sir. In your command."

General Arnold smiled at all of them. "He's in a good position, Mrs. Fraser. I can almost guarantee he won't be killed in the West Point garrison."

Jock broke in with a question about the battle of Saratoga, and the General seemed pleased to tell him about it. And by the time the great man rode away toward King's Ferry, Jock was his most devoted admirer.

Who could believe that the great General Arnold not only came to talk with Pa about gun repair, but sat in their kitchen eating Ma's food and talking with all of them just like—well, just like one of the neighbors in the valley? As far as Jock was concerned, General Arnold was a bigger hero even than General Washington. After all, General Washington had never visited Fraser Forge.

"I wager he'll win the war for us, some day," he said, in the middle of conversation the next day.

"Who?" His mother stared at him. She had been saying how hard it was to get along without sugar these days, and how she couldn't make gingerbread at all without molasses.

"General Arnold, of course."

"Oh, you and your General Arnold!" Peggy was disgusted. "Why, he's an old man, compared to Major André."

"But Major André is a Redcoat," Jock cried. "How can you keep thinking like that about a Redcoat?"

Peggy smiled demurely and lifted teasing blue eyes to say practically, "Why should I think of someone like General Arnold who's married?"

Dick Conway had been busy eating. Maggie's food was the best he'd ever eaten, and he'd been hungry for two years before he came to the Frasers. But he was filled up enough now to lay down his fork and join in the conversation.

"General Arnold married a Tory," he announced.

Jock looked at him as if he'd knifed his own mother.

"How can you say a thing like that?" He was outraged.

"Why, everyone in Philadelphia knows that! I was there, when General Arnold took command, and there was a lot of talk about him. Everyone said he was spending more money than any American general ever got paid."

Jock pushed his mouth out in stubborn protest.

"Some people just don't like heroes, I guess. Or else Philadelphia was full of Tories and they wanted to make trouble for a Patriot general."

Dick looked cynical. "Some people thought he was thinking a lot more about Arnold than about the Continental army. Some people said he was more interested in money than glory, even." He shrugged. "I don't say it's true. But that's what I heard while I was in Philadelphia."

"I don't believe a word of it." Jock slammed his fist down on the table in protest and glared at Dick. "You just believe all those stories about one of our heroes because you're British—and jealous." He had the horrid feeling Dick enjoyed annoying him.

"Well—he married one of the Shippen girls—the same one Major André was courting while Howe was in Philadelphia. Lots of people said the way she was carrying on with the British she must be an outright Loyalist."

George Fraser got interested in Dick's remarks.

"Arnold's a man that thinks pretty well of himself," he observed. "Maybe too well. Anybody talks so much about what he's done ain't really sure he's done it."

Jock felt his throat choking up. He couldn't bear to hear another word against General Arnold.

"What's wrong with a gentleman and a hero living like

a gentleman?" he demanded. He got up and rushed away from the table. But he couldn't help hearing Dick's last remark with a cynical laugh behind it: "There's nothing wrong with living like a gentleman, if you've got the money. If you haven't—well, then, where's it coming from?"

Jock left the hateful voices behind him and flung himself out of the house. Cartwright's offer tantalized him again. It returned at unexpected times. Money makes the man, he thought angrily. If Pa had the money he ought to have, he wouldn't be worrying about either rent or gun barrels . . . Without it he couldn't even be a craftsman . . .

He pushed his way through underbrush and tangles of vines on Teller's Point to the bluff overlooking the Hudson, and dropped to the ground, staring at the river, while he pursued his argument with himself. So why shouldn't General Arnold have money to live with, to fight with? He was winning the war for the colonies. Any general ought to have money. Why ask these ridiculous questions about where it came from?

The late afternoon was crystal-clear, and somewhere up the river something was going on. Jock focused his gaze, and then he ran back to the house, unseen, found his telescope and sped back to the point of land jutting into the river.

A stream of men was crossing the ferry at Stony Point, group by group, forming into companies and marching

A stream of men was crossing the ferry

off from Verplanck's Landing. This must be Washington's army, leaving Kakiat. A man on horseback stood at the Stony Point landing, watching the last detachment move across the water. Another horseman approached him. Staring at the tiny figures, enlarged enough in the telescope to show as people, Jock knew the one on the black horse was General Arnold.

He sat there, still as stone, his eye glued to the telescope. That should show people like Dick Conway: General Washington and General Arnold were meeting and talking like friends. Jock's hero sat his horse proud and straight, his head up, as he talked to General Washington, who was on a white horse.

At this distance, Jock thought, General Arnold looked the greater of the two. You could tell from his carriage. Pa had called him arrogant. But it wasn't arrogance, it was pride. And didn't General Arnold have a better right to be proud than any man in the Continental army?

Chapter 11

A FEW days later General Benedict Arnold had been appointed to the command of West Point. He would make his headquarters in the Beverly Robinson house, across from West Point and two miles downstream.

Jock, dreaming endlessly of ways and reasons to see General Arnold again, wondered if he might be able to order gun barrels delivered to Fraser Forge to fulfill the army contracts. When he mentioned this idea to his father in the forge, one day, George Fraser said he thought it was hardly likely General Arnold could find any iron that he himself had not already considered and tried to get. And Dick Conway laughed jeeringly at the very idea.

Dick was getting above himself, Jock thought, highly irritated with the boy he himself had brought to the forge. Dick had all these unfavorable opinions about General Arnold, and he kept teasing Jock about hero-worship. Well, Jock wanted to know, what was wrong with admiring a hero?

"Nothing," Dick said in a superior tone. "The only trouble is admiring someone who isn't a hero."

This kind of remark threw Jock into a rage. Once he swung violently at Dick in a fit of temper, and the English boy diverted the blow easily and laid Jock on the floor hard enough so Jock ached for a week. After that he held in his temper. But he spoke to Dick as little as possible.

The most aggravating thing of all was the way his father admired the apprentice's work.

"Best workman I've seen since I left Scotland," he said to Maggie once, not seeing Jock in the corner of the kitchen. "When this blasted war is over and we can get iron again, we'll make the finest guns at this forge that can be found in the country. He'll be one of the best gunsmiths I've ever seen."

Jock never let on he had overheard this praise for the boy he was coming to dislike intensely. But he couldn't forget it. Pa had never said anything like that about him. He was beginning to feel it would make no difference to Pa if he weren't even around. If old man Cartwright wasn't such a strong Tory, Jock would have run off and signed indentures with him, after all. And he brooded about some of his wrongs, until they seemed overwhelming.

When he was melancholy and sure that everyone around him thought he was stupid, he would think about the Ferguson gun. Just to handle it, run his fingers across the rich silver mounting, feel the smooth action of the loading device under his fingers could revive his spirits as nothing else could do. He had a hunger to carry it and shoot with it.

And when Dick was busy in the forge, Jock would slip out sometimes and return to the house, take the Ferguson out of its hiding place and handle it caressingly, dreaming of the time when he could have a gun like that for himself.

Once when he came down from the room in the loft where Dick slept, he met his mother coming in from the well with a bucket of water.

"What are you doing here at this time of day?" she wanted to know.

"I wasn't busy for a few minutes, and I wanted to see something."

She looked at him suspiciously, and he wondered if anything showed in his face.

"Did you see that gun Dick brought with him, when he came here?" He couldn't help asking the question, and Maggie looked at him sharply.

"Your pa showed it to me the night the boy came. He told Dick to keep it hidden away. It's too good a gun to take chances with. Why?"

Jock shrugged. "I just hope I can have one like it some day."

"Your pa will make some when he can get the parts again." She turned on him purposefully. "Don't you ever touch that gun, Jock. Mind what I say. It could never be replaced, if anything happened to it. Pa doesn't even want Dick to shoot it around here for fear someone will find out about it. Just forget there is such a gun."

"Aw, Ma! What do you think I am? Stupid?"

He felt very righteous. All he needed to know was that the gun was still in its hiding place. He was just as concerned about it as Pa was. He knew how important it was. . . .

And then he would recall that if Dick hadn't come, they would never have known about the Ferguson rifle. And if Dick should leave, the Ferguson would go with him. Jock writhed unhappily. He would have to get along with Dick, at least till Pa could find gun barrels and locks, and time to make the new gun.

It was the first week in September, and the hills glowed with the coming autumn, the loveliest season in the valley. But September first had been another rent day, gone by without money.

One of the farmers up the road had been snatched from his family by a gang who said they were Cartwright's police. A neighbor came by to tell the Frasers about it.

"The poor man couldn't pay the rent this past year, because the British army took everything he raised last year, and the American army took it this year." She lifted her hands and her eyes dramatically. "He was glad enough to help feed those poor boys in Washington's army. And even then they don't get enough to eat. All he had left was enough for his own family, and he offered the last barrel of flour to the old man on the hill, but it wasn't enough." Then she said ominously, "Makes you wonder who's going to win this war, when Tories can act so mean."

The quartermaster's aide who came by to pick up the musket he had left for repair said, "These Loyalists are acting as if they thought the British army was going to march through here any minute. Makes you think something's going on."

Jock asked the Skinners that night what they thought about the soldier's report.

"Cowboys sure seem confident these days," one of the men said. "They act like something's going to happen—coming up closer to the Croton lately than I've seen in a long time . . ."

On September 16 Rob came home for a five-day leave, and the first thing Jock wanted to know was, "How's General Arnold?"

Rob shook his head. "He isn't around all that much. He sent two hundred of the men way up the river to cut firewood for next winter, and he's got another couple hundred on guard at Fishkill. Nobody knows why."

"Well, you do need firewood in the winter, don't you? And how're you going to get it, if the men don't lay it in at a time like this when they're just sitting around with nothing to do?" Jock didn't like the criticism in Rob's tone.

"Oh, it don't bother me none," Rob said. "It was nice to be out in the woods in this weather. Only there's still a lot of work to be done on the walls of the fort. I'd think we'd do that before we go out for firewood."

"General Arnold stopped here about a month ago," Jock said. "I think he's the greatest general in the army!" His eyes glowed. "How does it feel to be under a general like him?"

Rob shrugged again. "Maybe he's great when he's leading an attack. But at West Point all we do is sit around."

"But it's the most important fort in this entire war!" Jock was affronted that Rob should consider his assignment so indifferently.

"What did he do about that chain?" George Fraser wanted to know.

Rob raised his eyebrows. "Couple officers keep bringing that up," he said. "So far he hasn't done anything. Not anything. Course, how do we know? Mebbe it doesn't need anything done. Again"—he paused and looked cynical—"maybe it does."

"I don't think you ought to have opinions like that about a man like him!" Jock cried.

"Hah! It's a free country!" Rob told his younger brother. "Anybody can have opinions about anyone, and I'm not sure about Arnold, no matter how many battles he's won."

But Rob was more worried about his father's situation than about West Point and Arnold.

"When this war is over you can buy this land," he assured his father. "Some of the Tory landlords in Pennsylvania had their property confiscated by the state, and sold to the people . . ."

"Question is how to stay here without rent till the war is won," George Fraser said pessimistically. "Mebbe if Arnold is sending companies of men in all directions he'd like to have a company down here guarding the Patriots on the Croton!" He laughed bitterly, as if he'd made a very funny joke.

But Jock told Rob later it was no joke at all. Cartwright's police were arresting tenants who had fallen behind in their rents, and he was afraid they'd come for Pa any time. He wanted Pa to run off and hide, and Pa wouldn't do it.

"Could you and Dick hold them off?" Rob demanded.

"If we was expecting them and ready for them," Jock said. "And if Dick was shooting with his Ferguson rifle gun. Only Pa keeps it hidden away so no one will know about it."

Rob shook his head. "Pa's a stubborn man," he said. "I just don't know . . ."

They went out to Teller's Point where they had built forts and played Indian wars years ago. The fort was now overgrown with grapevines. Rob stared at it incredulously. He always remembered it as being very much bigger.

He pulled off a cluster of rich blue grapes and ate them as he and Jock made their way to the bluff overlooking the river. There he stared at the ship at anchor in the bay, north of the point, frowning.

"I don't like the way the *Vulture* stays so far up the river," he said. "I've got a feeling I ought to get back to West Point."

"But your leave isn't up till tomorrow . . ."

"I know. But I ought to be there. Matter of fact, I thought it was funny to get leave when I did."

"But why? British boats go up and down all the time. Why would the *Vulture* mean anything more than a scouting trip?"

Rob shook his head. "That's what I don't know. Mebbe it doesn't mean anything. But mebbe it means an attack at the Point, and General Arnold is going to need every man he's got. I'll feel better if I get back."

In the sweet September sunshine, with the leaves just beginning to glow golden against the granite hills, the Frasers watched Rob set off up the rutted dusty road going north. He would be back at the Point before sundown on September 20.

He stared at the ship at anchor in the bay

Chapter 12

THERE was work to be done in the forge after Rob left. Half a dozen old muskets had come in the next morning.

"Militia want to pick them up tonight," Jock's father said. "Gotta work fast to get them ready."

Jock picked up the one nearest him and sat down to find out why the flintlock failed to fire the powder. The cover on the priming pan had jammed because of a bent hinge. He began to work with it and the cover snapped off altogether, and then he had to weld it. What a clumsy old piece, he thought in disgust.

But as he got into the work he became interested in spite of himself in doing a finer job of workmanship on the mended cover than the original workman had done. The cover snapped into place as smoothly as it should, the trigger tripped the sear perfectly. When he had done the work himself, there was some pleasure in firing even the old Brown Bess.

He set it down and picked up the next one. The trigger wouldn't pull, and he began to dismantle it. The tumbler had been forced out of alignment by a mainspring that had pulled apart. A job like this one took at least two hours, and his thoughts ran along as he worked, trying to see exactly how the old gunlock could be redesigned for top-loading, so the trigger guard might open a loading space.

He stood the old musket on its butt, bit open the cartridge of powder, and rammed it and the ball into place for test firing. The long ramrod stood almost as tall as he did, and must be fitted alongside the musket, which must be loaded, thus, always in a standing position. But the gun fired accurately, and, pleased, he stood it with the other gun and began work on another.

Dick was working on a long rifle, the finest gun made in the colonies. Jock had been pleased enough with his own long rifle until he saw the Ferguson. The long rifle stood some six inches taller than the Ferguson, and the ball, wrapped in an oiled patch of cloth, had to be rammed in from the muzzle. A man had to stand up to load the rifle, and at the most could repeat fire only a couple of times a minute.

But the Ferguson! Jock's thoughts went back to that jewel of a gun again. You could load the Ferguson lying flat on the ground, riding horseback; you could load it in the middle of the night.

The day was darkening earlier, already, than it had a week ago. As the sun slipped down the sky and the shadows became longer, Pa was still finishing the last gun barrel: it had burst, and had to be replaced, cooled, polished, tested.

"You go on in and get the firewood and water for your ma," he told Jock.

Dick began to clean up the forge for the night, and Jock sauntered slowly across the open space toward the house. Horses' hoofs sounded somewhere along one of the roads, and he wondered if the Cowboys were raiding near the Croton again.

The riders were alarmingly close and Jock froze to attention, with the load of firewood in his arm. Then he relaxed. It was quiet out by the forge, and if the men had stopped there, they probably were bringing guns for mending.

And then he heard his father yelling, "You blasted Tories! Get out of my place and stay out!"

There were angry yells and shots, and a sudden barrage of shooting from the river. Jock hesitated a moment, wondering about the armed sloop down there, and then about Pa. He dropped the load of wood on the floor and dashed out the door to the forge.

"Jock! Where's your gun?" his mother called after him.

When he reached the forge it was empty. The newly tested gun barrel lay on the floor with a footprint showing on the brown metal. No one was there. The sound of hoofs was fading away somewhere to the north, although another barrage of shooting from the river confused Jock even about the direction of the hoofbeats. He raced back to the house.

"Ma! He's gone. And Dick's gone, too."

His mother looked white. But she never wavered. "Was it Cartwright's men?"

"I don't know, Ma. I heard him yell at Tories."

She shook her fist in the direction of the iron plantation. Then, "You going out with the Skinners tonight, Jock?"

"Fast as I can get there."

"Take along something to eat." Ma was fitting bread and meat together and stuffing them into the pockets of his coat. "It might be a long night. You say Dick is gone, too?"

"Nobody was in the forge at all, when I got there."

"Will the Skinners take out and look for your pa?"

"They sure will."

He picked up his rifle, and then stopped. The Ferguson would be ever so much easier to use, on a search like this. Dick would be the first to urge him to carry a good weapon. . . . He took the Ferguson out of its hiding place and ran down the steep steps from the loft, two at a time.

"Jock! You taking that gun?" His mother stopped him with a firm hand.

"Ma, this is the only decent gun on the place. If I'm going to get Pa out of Cartwright's jail, or wherever he is, I can't do it without a good gun."

Over her protest, he ran out the door, saddled Ginger, and set off to meet the Skinners at Turley Venner's house, up the Croton River, near the bridge.

Venner's farm was in an isolated spot with secret lanes leading into the roads to North Castle, White Plains, and Tarrytown. Venner had three boys in the Continental armies. He and his wife lived alone, farming their crops as best they could, and holding off the raiding Cowboys.

Mrs. Venner was a skinny, aging woman who could throw an axe as accurately as any Indian could hurl a tomahawk, and Skinners still laughed about how she had been surprised in her dairy by a marauding trio of Cowboys. She had cloven the skull of one with a hatchet, and screaming like a banshee, had chased the other two straight into the Croton River.

He set off on Ginger, gun in hand, to meet the Skinners

Twenty Skinners were collected at the Venner house when Jock got there. Most of them he knew. He was still the youngest one of the group, and he had an uneasy feeling that they looked on him as a youngster, a boy who was tagging along.

But tonight he was carrying the Ferguson. Nobody had a gun like this one. They would have to respect him now.

They were arguing when he got there about whether they should head straight into Cowboy territory and avenge the latest Cowboy raid, or whether they should hit the Cartwright ironworks.

"Time someone went after the old Tory," one man cried. "He took pore old Farmer Pitkin a couple days ago for the rent money."

"They got Pa tonight," Jock announced, as soon as he could be heard.

The group swung toward him. "What? Kidnaped Fraser? When did this happen?"

Jock told the story. "I heard my father yell 'Get off the place you Tories' . . . He was behind in the rent because Cartwright stopped selling iron to him."

"Any idea which way they went?"

"There was some shooting on the river right then. By the time it stopped I couldn't hear the horses any more. They coulda gone in any direction."

"Musta been when we were firing on the boat from the *Vulture*," one of the men said, looking up from under shaggy brows. "What's that British boat doing at Teller's Point anyway?"

"Who knows? Maybe we oughta chase it down tonight?"

Jock wondered if they were going to forget his father, with so many inviting ways to make trouble, and he balanced his gun in both hands to impress them a little.

"Hey, look at the gun the kid's got!" That was Mogan. He was a black-haired ruffian, brawny and dirty, whom Jock had seen only once before. He reached over and picked up the Ferguson. "Where'd you get a gun like this?"

He balanced it, admired it, turning it over, sighting along the barrel. Jock began to swell up with satisfaction.

"It's a Ferguson," he said. "I'll show you how it works. It's the greatest rifle gun we ever saw at our place."

He showed them the loading device, the turn of the trigger guard; he raised it and pulled the trigger, demonstrating how a man could shoot eight bullets a minute. Only, being out of practice, he explained, the best he could do was five a minute.

Mogan took it from him again and tried it himself. "Hey, now!" he cried in admiration. "A man could win a war with that kind of gun! Got any bullets? I want to try this on a target!"

"Aw, it's too dark!"

Mogan guffawed. "You could hit a target in the dark with this baby!"

Fear suddenly ran down Jock's spine with a chilling touch. Mogan was much too interested in the Ferguson. And as if a light had gone on too late, Jock saw with sharp terror why Pa had said he should show this gun to no one. He had known all along, he acknowledged wretchedly to himself. How could he have been so stupid tonight?

He tried to act as if he were not even noticing Mogan's interest in the Ferguson.

"Do you think we can find my pa, Mr. Venner?" he asked loudly.

Venner nodded and raised his voice. "Hey, boys! Ain't we going to get our gunsmith back again?"

"You bet we'll get him back!" they yelled with enthusiasm, eyes on the new rifle gun.

Venner howled for quiet. "They coulda taken him straight to New York," he reminded the gang. "If they did, they're still on the road. Jock, you go with my patrol and we'll go up to Cartwright's place."

Mogan yelled, "Boys! My gang will take the White Plains Road!"

To Jock's horror and disbelief, Mogan ran out of the door, still carrying the Ferguson, and his patrol swept away before the boy could even cry out for the gun.

Chapter 13

Jock followed Venner with his patrol of twelve men, overcome with panic. His father would feel worse about the loss of the Ferguson rifle than about his own imprisonment.

Jock had picked up, reluctantly, the old Brown Bess musket that Mogan had left on the floor of the meeting room when he had run off with the Ferguson. Now he berated himself for being fool enough not to ride off with Mogan's patrol, instead of Venner's. Why, he demanded of himself over and over, had he left the man?

So he rode, moping and sullen, at the end of the line. Ahead of him half a dozen men muttered in laughing undertones about finding their gunsmith, beating down the jail and taking him home in triumph. But Jock could hardly wish his father found before he got the Ferguson gun back again.

After an hour or so he began to recover his wits. He kicked his horse into a faster pace and pulled up alongside the man in front of him. This was a slovenly, rough-looking young man named Isaac Van Wart. He rode with his head poked forward, carrying a long rifle ready to fire.

Jock could see him looking from one side of the road to the other, and had the feeling Van Wart could see things in the darkness that he could not see. In spite of the man's raggedness and grime, his presence was comforting, because it seemed as if he could smell danger before it menaced them. After a quarter mile Van Wart sagged back in his saddle, as if some danger was past.

"Mr. Van Wart?" the boy whispered.

"Hey?"

"Can you give me some advice?"

Van Wart gave a rough whispering chuckle. "Sure, boy. What kin I tell you?"

"Do you remember that Ferguson rifle gun I was carrying when I came tonight?"

"Yep. Nice gun."

"Well, Mr. Mogan was looking at it and he ran off with it when he took his patrol out."

"So?" The question was flat and cold.

Suffocating panic was crowding Jock's throat again. "Do you think I can get it back?"

Van Wart spat into the undergrowth along side the road. "Wal, I dunno, boy. How come you let it get outa yore hands?"

In the dark, Jock's cheeks were flaming with humiliation.

"He wanted to see how it worked. And I guess maybe he forgot to give it back to me when he started out."

"He didn't forget," Van Wart said.

They rode along in silence. The hoofbeats of other horses in other lanes sounded in the night. But Venner was not chasing stray hoofbeats tonight. He was leading his patrol toward the bridge where the road led straight on to the big hill.

"That was a pretty good gun, eh?" Van Wart startled Jock with his question.

"Yes, it was a good gun. Besides, it wasn't mine. I've got to get it back, Mr. Van Wart. I can't go home without it."

Van Wart nodded slowly, as if his thoughts were working along an unknown route. He spat again.

"Will we meet Mogan's patrol at the end of the night?" Jock asked.

"Nope. Everybody scatters for his watch, and then they just go home at dawn."

Jock's courage seemed to ebb right out through his feet. He felt as if he wanted to die right there in the dark lane.

"Look, Mr. Van Wart. That gun is almost as important as finding Pa. Do you know where Mr. Mogan lives? Could we go to his house tonight and get it back?"

Van Wart was thinking very hard, and this took all his attention. Then, "Would that gun fire regular balls?"

"Nope. Wrong gauge."

Van Wart was silent again while he put these facts together. "If he ain't got any ammunition, he can't fire the gun. Can he now?"

"I guess not."

Van Wart nodded. "Mebbe he'll want back his own gun by the end of the night. A gun he can fire."

"Do you think so?"

"If it was me, I would."

Jock began to feel better. He sat up straighter and began to pay attention to his surroundings.

"Can you fire that old Bess?" Van Wart asked.

"He didn't leave any bullets with it." Jock felt almost like laughing. Van Wart reached into one big baggy pocket and pulled out a handful of cartridges. "Reckon these would fit? If you hafta fire that gun tonight you better be ready."

Jock opened the leather pouch that hung on his belt and dropped in the ammunition. "Thanks."

The woods had closed in again, the path had narrowed, and Jock let his horse drop back into single file. An hour later Van Wart said, "Mogan lives down near Pugsley's Point."

It was nearly midnight when they came out on the river road again. The starlight reflected from the water was almost as bright as moonlight, and the troop stopped in a little grove of trees, to hear Venner's orders.

"Now we're going to ride single file into there, and keep it quiet, boys. Jock, you know where the jail would be?"

"Yessir."

"You lead the men."

Jock led the men into a clearing and pointed

He set off into a lane that led around back of the hill where the ironmaster's mansion stood. There was a stone building hidden in the woods some quarter mile back of the house, where Cartwright kept unruly tenants and rebellious slaves. Jock led the twelve men into a clearing and pointed ahead. "There's the jail."

As he spoke, a guard called, "Who goes there?"

"Captain Venner, New York State Militia."

"Take your men away, Captain. Nobody interferes with this guardhouse."

"Do you hold a gunsmith named Fraser?"

There was a short silence. Then, "Never heard of him."

"What prisoners do you hold?"

"Couple of runaway apprentices." The guard's tone changed. "Get going!" His musket sounded, and a bullet plowed the dust near Jock's horse. Ginger shied violently.

Venner hesitated. Suddenly half a dozen muskets sounded. In the explosions Jock could see the ring of men around the jail. Half of them were loading muskets, the others were aiming at the little group of Skinners.

"Get away, men." Venner spoke sharply. "Fade into the woods. Don't try to stay together. Get back across the river."

Another volley of musket fire exploded, and one of the men sagged forward upon his horse, howling with pain and anger. Venner grabbed his rein. "Hang on!" he ordered, leading the way into the covering trees at the far edge of the clearing.

Jock followed at his heels. The wounded man frightened Jock into a panic, and when he found himself again in the dark lane leading to the bridge over the Croton, he began to shake so he could hardly sit his horse. He thought about General Arnold and felt ashamed. But that didn't stop the shaking.

Back in the Neutral Ground, the patrol came together again.

"How about that, Venner?" one of the men demanded. "Can we break into that guardhouse or not?"

Venner shook his head angrily. "Somebody musta

warned him. We'll have to figure out another way. I'd like to scare the old man himself."

"He's got more guards than Skinners and Cowboys put together," one of the men cried. The others laughed at the joke on themselves. Jock was still frightened and hating himself for it. The wounded man was groaning.

"Meet tomorrrow night at Jennings' place near Sing Sing," Venner said. "We'll need more men. Come on, boys, let's get Joe here home and to bed."

He wheeled his horse around and started up the road with the injured man's horse following. Jock sat still. He'd better stick with Van Wart, since he hoped the man would go with him to Mogan's house in the morning.

They took the wounded man home. Then Van Wart demanded, "You gonna keep sentry watch with me? Then you can go along home in the morning. We're short now, with Joe hurt."

"I can't go home," Jock said. He felt very sorry for himself, but he followed Van Wart's clumsy farm horse through paths and lanes until they arrived at the barn where Van Wart was assigned to watch.

They crawled into the hayloft and huddled the hay around them for warmth. Van Wart stationed himself at one window, whence he could watch the road. Jock took another window and thought he was watching alertly. The black pastures and ruined houses were still. He never knew when he fell asleep.

Then the air was full of gunfire, and Jock came to himself with a start, sitting bolt upright and wondering why he was in this strange barn covered with hay. Cannon fire resounded somewhere in the distance. Van Wart moved a little.

Outside, the fresh wind shook drying leaves from the trees, and the sky was pinkening slowly in the east. Somewhere to the north guns sounded steadily.

"What's all the noise about?" Van Wart grumbled, rousing himself. Then, "Now it's daylight we might's well go along and find something to eat."

They crept outside the barn, watching for spying eyes, washed at the well, and mounted their horses. The bombardment grew heavier, the puffs of smoke and flashes of explosions showed above the trees up the river. Must be at Teller's Point, Jock figured. Must be shelling the *Vulture*.

"That's a good thing," Van Wart said placidly, as they rode over to the river to watch the exploding shells. "That ship's got no business there in Haverstraw Bay. Oughta get her outa there." He looked at Jock. "You getting hungry?"

He was wishing Jock would invite him to ride to the Fraser house not far away for something to eat, and Jock suddenly remembered why he was here with Van Wart in the chilly dawn.

"I'm sure hungry," he said. "But I can't go home without that gun."

His companion sighed. "Best you come along to my place, then." He lived in the Neutral Ground in a squalid shack with his mother, and they rode almost an hour to reach it.

The shelling went on until eight o'clock, when it ended with a massive explosion.

"Something blew up," Van Wart said. "Eat up, Jock, and we'll go over and see what's going on."

The oatmeal was lumpy and unsalted. But it was filling, and Jock emptied his bowl.

"Can we go over to Mogan's place now?" he asked.

The reached the bluff and saw the *Vulture* in full sail, heading downstream.

"Now what was that sloop doing so far upstream?" Van Wart kept asking himself in a puzzled tone. Jock was curious about it, but not so much as about the Ferguson.

"Do we take this road to Mogan's place?" he asked, turning his horse's head toward the south.

"Might's well go there," Van Wart conceded, riding beside him. "Nothing else to do today, 'cept figure out how to get your pa."

Jock had never ridden through the Neutral Ground in broad daylight before, and he was shocked at the devastation.

"That used to be the Smith farm." Van Wart pointed to the blackened buildings on the right. "Cowboys drove all their cattle off couple of months ago, and then came back and burned the buildings. The Smiths went to New

York. They ain't Tories, but they said they'd feel safer there anyway."

Half mile further on, "There's the Van Dyke place. Cowboys kidnaped old Van Dyke for ransom last June, and by the time he got back they'd taken all his cattle. Course, he was a Tory anyway. Even the Tories can't work a farm around here, with the Cowboys stealing anything that moves."

"I guess you're lucky they don't bother your place," Jock ventured.

"They don't bother us!" Van Wart let out a guffaw. "Ma can handle a gun as well as I can. She got one of them right through the forehead once, and they been leaving us alone since."

The Mogan place looked even more run-down than the surrounding farms. Van Wart hollered from the road, while still on his horse. To Jock he said, "Everybody's suspicious these days. It's better not to knock on the door till he sees who it is."

Mogan stood in the open door, barefooted and bleary-eyed.

"Oh, Van Wart. Come along, Isaac. What's on your mind this morning?"

"Bill, Jock here says you got his gun by mistake last night, and he's brought yours along to trade back."

Mogan looked threatening. "What gun's he talking about?"

Van Wart leveled his own gun at him. "New kind of

rifle. But there warn't no ammunition to go with it."

"Oh, that one! I wondered what happened to my good shooting gun."

"The kid took it along, when you took his. He'll give it back when he gets his own."

Mogan scratched his head, looking foolish. "I reckon I left it somewhere last night."

"Well, that's a pretty stupid way to handle somebody's gun! Where'd you go last night?"

"Last thing I remember was Mead's Tavern, up back of Cartwright's place."

"I thought you was going down White Plains Road."

"We rode clear to White Plains, and there wasn't a soul stirring last night. So we rode back up to Mead's to consider what to do next."

Van Wart turned to Jock. "Well, kid, I guess we'll haveta ride up to Mead's Tavern for that gun. You just keep the musket you got till we get back the other one."

"What am I going to do without a gun?" yelled Mogan. "Gimme that musket! What if the Cowboys come around here and I got no gun?"

"You shoulda thought of that last night," Van Wart told him. "We'll bring this one back when we find t'other one."

He wheeled his horse and turned into the lane going north. Jock followed him, feeling now that the Ferguson rifle was gone for good.

Chapter 14

"I don't know about riding to Mead's in broad daylight," Van Wart said, as they rode away from Mogan's house. "Might be better if we waited till tonight. Daylight you never know who's waiting to pick you off."

Jock said nothing. He was trying to think of something he could do for himself, without waiting for Van Wart to think of something. In fact, he was beginning to wish he could get rid of Van Wart, who was a very tiresome companion.

But Van Wart had nothing better to do today than ride around, and he was enjoying Jock's company.

"I figure we might as well git into the Tarrytown Road and watch for someone going through," he said, looking as nearly eager as he ever did. "No use waiting around near the Croton. No Loyalists roaming around up here."

At the next fork he nudged Jock to follow him, and turned left, following a path that led into the Tarrytown Road and then south again. Jock stayed with him because he could think of nothing better to do. He thought about General Arnold. What would a hero do, in Jock's kind of trouble?

"We can't do no good for your pa till we get the rest of the patrol with us," Van Wart went on, as if he were thinking out loud. "Daytimes all we can do is lie low and catch some traveler going to New York. Someone like that usually has money on him . . . If Mead's got your gun, he'll keep it. We ought to have some of the boys with us. I've known Mead to shoot a raider without even asking what side he's on."

He stopped at a lonely farmhouse and asked for bread and cheese for the two of them. The farm wife glared at him, but with her mouth clamped tightly shut she set out bread and cheese. Then she said in tones of loathing, "That's all there is in the house! It's all we can do to feed ourselves, without having to feed every begging Skinner comes to the door!"

Van Wart snorted with laughter and carried the food out to a spreading oak tree on the far side of the road.

"We get used to the farmers complaining about the Skinners," he said, as if it amused him. "But what do they expect? If we weren't patrolling, the Cowboys would strip them of everything. I don't guess a little food is too much to pay for protection!"

The day was more bearable for Jock, when he had some food in his stomach. But it dragged intolerably, nonetheless. It seemed as if the Ferguson rifle were receding farther from him with the passing hours. And as

He carried the food out to a spreading oak

the sun went down and the chill night winds rose, he wondered miserably if he could ever go home again.

The Skinners met that night at Jennings' house near Sing Sing, deep in the Neutral Ground. Tonight Mogan was not there. Van Wart and Jock were the only men from the night before, and Jock was so tired of Van Wart's company that he would have liked to join a different group. But on the other hand, Van Wart knew now where the Ferguson was, and it might be dangerous for any of the others to know about it.

While his thoughts were following this reasoning, the captains of the patrols were lining out the assignments. Van Wart nudged him with a sharp elbow, and Jock came out of his thoughts with a painful jolt. "We're going north tonight," Van Wart said. "Mebbe we can stop at Mead's and pick up that gun."

The men set off as they had the night before, and Jock went with the patrol riding north. Mead's Tavern was a long way from the Neutral Ground, up beyond Crompond, and he wondered how many would care to go so far. He glanced at the stars: it was already getting on toward nine o'clock. Jock settled back in his saddle and let his horse go on a loose rein: with four ahead and seven behind him, Ginger would not get off the road, and Jock let his head drop and dozed a little.

He stopped with a jerk and came wide awake. When he looked at the stars, it was hard to believe he had lost so much time. They were on the North Castle Road, somewhere beyond Pines Bridge, and the men were listening to a uniformed captain of the regular militia.

"A party came along this way an hour ago," the captain was saying. "You might want to look out for them tomorrow. Two men and a servant. I have a feeling they're Loyalists."

"Where are they now, Captain?"

In the starlight the smile on the captain's face was sinister.

"I sent them over to Lane's farmhouse for the night. They wanted to ride straight through to White Plains tonight—and they seemed to think they didn't have to worry about Cowboys. That's why you can keep an eye out for them. By the time I asked a few questions, they decided not to go any farther tonight. But keep your eyes open, just the same."

"Which way will they go in the morning, Captain?"

"They want to get to White Plains. But cover the Tarrytown Road as well. They might change their minds." He paused as if he were trying to recall something important. Then he said, "I might have stopped them myself, I suppose. But I was alone and could find no real reason to stop them . . . and yet . . . one of them was a Joshua Smith, said he had a brother in New York, and that General Arnold employed him to see the gentlemen with him safely through to White Plains . . . And then Smith said he might not go all the way himself—" The captain evidently wanted to recall why he felt suspicious about the men. "I'll tell you, boys. The gentleman with Smith wore a purple coat with gold lace and white-top riding boots. But he rode like an officer. If you stop him somewhere, it might be worthwhile."

The militia captain rode off and the captain of the Skinner patrol said, "Might be money here, men. Let's cover both roads in the morning. Who wants to take the White Plains Road with me?"

Three men offered to meet him on the White Plains Road somewhere below Pleasantville, and they rode off to agree on their meeting place.

The seven who were left looked at each other. The travelers would take one road or the other.

"Pickings been pretty thin lately," Van Wart said. "I'll be at the bridge down near Tarrytown in the morning. Anybody wants to join me, all right. If nobody comes, I can take care of this yere company of three by myself!"

The possibility of loot was so fascinating that for the next hour they debated whether to do anything further that night at all. Things were quiet, one of them argued. No Cowboys around. Not enough of them in this patrol to attack Cartwright's jail again.

"The kid here had his gun stolen, and we're going to ride up to Mead's Tavern and look for it," Van Wart said.

"What kind of gun?" A skinny blond man with a bad complexion sounded much too interested.

"Aw, a new kind of rifle. Jock's pa is a gunsmith, and if we get him back and the gun, mebbe he'll make us each a gun like it."

This was persuasion enough, and without further argument, the band turned north again, to ride up to Mead's Tavern.

By the time they got there it was very late, and the tavern was dark. Van Wart pounded on the door with his gun butt.

"Open up here!" he bawled.

A window opened above the door, and a head in a nightcap showed itself. "What do you ruffians want at this hour of the night?"

Jock looked up. The white nightcap was a blur in the darkness. But the glint of starlight on the barrel of the rifle was clear.

"Don't shoot!" he called. "We're friends."

"Friends don't hammer down the door in the middle of the night. Be off with you, 'fore I do shoot."

While they hesitated, uncertain whether to break in or not, the rifle spat, and the horses shied as a bullet plowed into the dust in their midst.

"Aw, Mead, don't lose your head!" Van Wart cried. "All we want is a drink to wet our whistles."

"Come around in the morning," Mead snapped. "And get going now, before I aim a bullet where it'll count."

He was ramming the bullet into the rifle barrel as he talked, and with another glance at each other, the seven

Skinners decided not to argue with him longer. They turned and galloped away into the night. Jock could hear the window sash squeaking painfully as the tavernkeeper slammed his window shut.

So the whole night had been a waste of time, Jock told himself, angry and dismal, as he rode away with the troop. He still couldn't go home. It was too late now to do anything but keep the watch. And probably tomorrow Mr. Mead would refuse again to let any Skinners into his tavern.

Beside him Van Wart said, with more cheerfulness than he had shown at any other time, "Well, we tried, Jock. Can't do more than try, can we?"

Jock shrugged. He was too melancholy to say anything.

"You come home with me tonight, and tomorrow we'll try again."

The boy burst out angrily. "We can't do anything in daylight, and then we can't do anything at night, either! I don't think I'll ever get that gun back again!"

"Aw, don't get so upset," Van Wart soothed him. "To-morrow morning anything can happen. But I'll tell you. We'll go back to Mead's tomorrow for sure. Before dark."

Jock was too tired to think about tomorrow. It was all he could do to hang onto his horse till he reached Van Wart's place.

Chapter 15

WHEN Jock opened his eyes in the morning, he felt as if he were doomed to spend the rest of his life in Van Wart's slovenly shack, far from home, with a man he was beginning to dislike intensely, in spite of his friendly help.

"What help?" Jock asked himself, as he plunged his head into cold water. Far as he could see, all they'd been doing for two days and nights was riding around for nothing. But he climbed on his horse after breakfast and followed Van Wart out of the shabby farmyard without a word.

"Cat get your tongue?" Van Wart inquired, with humorous solicitude.

Jock muttered something about not feeling real good, and fell behind his companion, when they entered the narrow path that led to the Tarrytown road. An hour later they came out into the sunlight on the open road, fifteen minutes' ride from Tarrytown.

Jock had never been so far south in the Neutral Ground, and he felt nervous. This was deep in enemy territory. Ahead of them the bridge where the road crossed the river showed gaps in the planking like broken teeth.

Five ragged men crawled out of the underbrush, looking rougher and dirtier than they had last night.

Van Wart said, "Boys, some of you can hide on that little rise over there. The rest of us will sit under the bridge. Who wants the hill?"

One of the ragged men said, "I like to be up where I can see what's coming and going." He turned his horse toward the little hill, and two of the others followed him.

Jock went with Van Wart to the bridge. His companions were John Paulding and David Williams, and Jock disliked both of them. Just as his pa had said, the Skinners were nothing but a gang of ruffians. But until Jock got the Ferguson in his hands again, he dared not lose track of Isaac Van Wart, nor anger him.

They tied their horses to small trees on the south side of the bridge, where they were somewhat hidden, and Van Wart pulled a deck of cards from his pocket.

"We'll draw to see who gets to play cards in the shade," he announced. "T'other two can watch the road. If nobody comes along before noon, we'll change around."

Williams drew a card and shook his head. He was a stupid-looking farm boy, with his front teeth hanging out, and he said almost nothing. Paulding drew his card briskly. He was wearing a Hessian coat, and while he made jokes about it, the uniform coat looked more fit than any of the clothes the other Skinners wore. He had been a prisoner in New York in the spring and had fooled one of the Hessian guards, who could speak no English, into letting him look at his gun. He had over-powered the guard, taken his coat, and escaped. This was the greatest exploit of his entire life, and he talked about it all the time.

Now he said, "I used to play cards with the Hessian guards all the time. Stupidest men I ever knew." Jock thought bitterly that must really be a record. He shook his head, when Van Wart held out the cards.

"I'd rather watch the road," he said.

When the three compared their cards, Van Wart's was low. In disgust he threw it down, the wind caught it, and Paulding, dragging the skirts of his long coat through the grass, scrambled after it.

"Come on, Jock," Van Wart said with humorous resig-nation. "We got the watch. Hope for a good haul."

The other two sat down under the bridge in the shade. Jock and Van Wart concealed themselves in the growth along the roadside, where they could see the road for half a mile. It was only a little after eight in the morn-ing, and Jock gritted his teeth when he thought of the day before him and the perversity of fate that kept him tied to Van Wart.

"When do you think we can go up to Mead's Tavern?" he asked his companion after half an hour.

"Oh, you still worried about that gun?"

"I don't want someone else to get it!" Jock exploded.

"Don't worry so much, kid. This whole war has been poking along for five years. You think you can pick up a lost gun in a coupla hours?"

Jock forced a smile. But he moved back from the road and threw himself flat on the grass behind the undergrowth, on his face.

"You all right?" Van Wart was solicitous. But even his concern was irritating, and Jock didn't answer.

The sun was warm on his back, the grass smelled like fresh hay, and he began to relax. He thought about going up to Mead's Tavern and reclaiming the gun by a heroic strategy that included pinning the tavernkeeper to the wall with the bayonet on the Brown Bess. That seemed too easy, and something always rose up in his mind and said clearly, "What are you going to do, if you don't get that Ferguson back?"

Well, he thought, in the peaceful quiet of the sunny field, maybe he'd run away from the Skinners, join Colonel Patrick Ferguson and the British army, and then, when he'd gotten another Ferguson gun, he could desert and make his way home again.

By the time he had worked out this program in some detail, including surrendering the entire British company to Benedict Arnold, he was feeling good again, and he rolled over and sat up. Van Wart was kneeling behind the bush near the road, staring into the distance with one hand shading his eyes.

"Someone coming?" Jock scrambled to his feet.

"Sh! Keep still and listen. Get down!"

The boy crouched where he could see the road. A man on horseback was approaching at a good pace.

"This will be our man," Van Wart said with satisfaction. "If he isn't the one the captain told us about, mebbe he'll be a bonus." Then, disappointed, "I thought there was three of them. This here is only one."

He sent Jock back to the bridge to warn the cardplayers, and as the horseman approached the bridge they slapped down their cards and scrambled out on the road to stop him. He was studying a small map as he rode, and for some moments he didn't notice the men waiting at the bridge. The three stationed on the hill rode down at top speed to join in the capture.

Something about the horseman was familiar to Jock, and the boy's heart began to beat hard and slow, while he stared at the rider. He was wearing the white-top boots and the purple coat with gold lace that the captain had described last night. And he rode, unarmed and alone, with a gallant gaiety.

When he saw the Hessian coat, the rider smiled as if he recognized friends.

"Gentlemen," he said sunnily, "I hope you belong to the lower party." This was the British force controlling the state below Tarrytown.

Van Wart glanced at Paulding with a slow wink. "We do," he said indifferently. "What's it to you?"

"So do I," said the rider. "I'm glad you're of my party,

because I'm a British officer on important business, and I must not be detained."

He pulled out a gold watch, as proof of his being an officer. And Jock's mind went back to a summer's day more than a year ago, when a debonair young British officer had drunk from their well, flirted with Peggy, and shown them his gold watch. He knew this man, and his breath caught painfully: Major John André, as handsome and confident as he had been a year ago . . . but out of uniform? Jock met Major André's eyes and smiled involuntarily.

The Major smiled back, and Jock felt trapped. The Major didn't remember him, but he thought the boy was a friend. Confused, Jock stepped back from the group questioning André, trying to think. He'd like to see him ride safely on. And yet, all the Skinners wanted was money. He should be safe enough . . .

"Well, now," Williams drawled, "let me see that watch and suppose you get off your horse and talk this over."

The rider glanced from one face to another, and his own became wary. He dismounted and faced them.

"I'm happy, gentlemen, to find I'm mistaken in your party. You must belong to the *upper* party, and so do I. After all, a man must use any shift he can to get through the Neutral Ground these days." He looked from one unsmiling face to another, looking for a response. "I'm in General Arnold's service, gentlemen. John Anderson is my name, and here is General Arnold's pass."

"Well, blow Arnold's pass," said Paulding, hardly glancing at it. "You said you're a British officer. Where's your money?"

"Gentlemen, I have no money with me."

"A British officer and no money?" Van Wart demanded caustically. "Come on, boys. We'll search him."

Jock watched them with a sick feeling. What did André mean, calling himself Anderson "in General Arnold's service?" Had he defected to the Americans? But still, he was in neither American nor British uniform . . . In Arnold's service? Spying for Arnold in disguise? Jock shook his head, too confused to know what to think, reaching for something hopeful.

"He'll have the money in his boots," cried Williams, when nothing was found in his clothing.

Watching the man closely, Jock sensed a recoil. He didn't want his boots searched. Probably the money was there, the boy told himself. Naturally he wouldn't want them to find it.

They pulled off his boots with a rude force that threw him to the ground, where he sat quietly, awaiting the end of the search. As the boots came off there was a sound of paper crackling, and they pulled off his socks as well, and found papers inside.

Van Wart unfolded them, looked them over hastily, tossed them to the ground. He could not read, and they contained no money. The Dutchman turned to search the saddlebags.

They pulled off his boots with a rude force

142

"Gentlemen," said the prisoner, sitting on the ground with his arms linked around his knees, "if you have such a thirst for money, I can put you in a way to get it."

"What will you give us to let you go?"

"Any sum you want," said André, with casual assurance. "A hundred guineas, with horse, saddle, bridle, and watch?"

"Yes, and I'll have the money sent here, if you wish."

Williams looked as if he had got hold of a game more fascinating than cards. "Would you give more?"

"A thousand guineas," the captive said promptly.

"Well . . ." They were half greedy, half curious to see how high he would go to buy his freedom.

"Ten thousand guineas," the man said, spreading out his hands to indicate that any sum, any sum at all, would be reasonable for safe delivery to his own lines.

Van Wart stared incredulously. "Who ever heard of ten thousand guineas?" he demanded, turning to his companions.

Paulding said, "What would you do if you had ten thousand guineas, Dave? Me, I'd buy a good horse, right off. And a fancy place like the ironmaster's, up there on the hill." He began to clown around, holding out the skirts of the Hessian coat. "Can't you see me in a velvet coat, sky blue, mebbe, with gold lace and a fancy hat?"

Jock froze in agonized attention. The Major meant what he said. Someone would pay so much money for his ransom—and only twenty or thirty silver guineas would pay the quitrent for George Fraser and set him free, buy the gun barrels he needed so badly . . . He was seeing the picture so clearly that he didn't hear the exchange of conversation for some minutes.

Van Wart was guffawing raspily. "If the ten thousand guineas was paper, you could hardly buy a good horse, John!"

"My good man, I'm talking about gold!" André exclaimed. "Take me to King's Bridge and I can pay you there."

"And what business would you have at King's Bridge?" Paulding demanded, suddenly sobered. "No, no, sir. If we took you to King's Bridge, we'd be delivered to the Sugar House prison, and you'd save your money!"

"If you won't trust my honor, six of you shall stay with me here, and one of you shall go with a letter I'll write. Name your sum." He looked from one to another, dead serious now.

At the note of desperation in the prisoner's voice, Jock came back to attention. This was a man of honor, he knew. If he said the money would be delivered, it would be theirs. He opened his mouth to speak up for the captive, and visions of gold glimmered before his eyes.

He was starting to say, "I know this man," when Paulding said, "You send a letter, and first thing we know a party will be out and take us all prisoners here."

"This is a man of honor," Jock cried. "I'll write such a letter, if you don't trust him!"

They all became silent, looking at Jock. He could sway this party, he knew. They wanted money badly enough to listen to him. He could save this prisoner—and collect thousands of gold guineas at the same time.

"I dunno how it's going to be safe," Van Wart said thoughtfully, scratching his head and staring at the prisoner. The papers tossed on the ground lifted in the wind, and fell against Jock's shoe. He picked them up, thinking they might contain something that would convince the Skinners that André might safely be delivered to King's Bridge for the ransom in gold.

The first paper was a memorandum about the defenses of West Point. The second one was a carefully drawn plan of the fortifications of the fort. Jock looked at the signature on the papers: it matched the signature on the pass. General Arnold had signed these papers, and Major André of the British army was carrying them to British army headquarters. Jock began to sweat.

Had they caught a spy? Had they come upon a plot to give West Point itself to the British? The prisoner had said he was "in General Arnold's service". A sob formed in Jock's throat, and he worked to swallow it.

He looked at his companions. They were all watching the business before them with greedy expressions. But Paulding had been a prisoner of war. He had fought for the rebel cause.

"Mr. Paulding, sir . . ."

Paulding looked around, impatient at the interruption.

The bidding for ransom had gone to twenty thousand gold guineas. Major André was sitting on the ground, his arms encircling his knees, looking up at his captors with the challenging air of one playing a sporting game.

Jock shut his mouth again.

He *liked* the man sitting there on the ground. He liked him much better than the ruffians who were detaining him. Suppose he said, "Men, I know this prisoner, and you need fear no treachery. He'll give us the gold."

The thought of his share in such a prize made him gulp. Maybe twenty-five hundred guineas—depending on where the bidding stopped. A fortune! And Pa was in jail for lack of twenty guineas!

Jock closed his eyes in an anguish of indecision. All he had to do, Jock thought, was to persuade his friends to let the British officer go. They could take his papers and his gold . . . That was all. Nothing more.

But Rob was in West Point. What would happen to Rob? What would happen to General Washington? What would happen to the colonies? He made up his mind, and spoke: "Mr. Paulding, sir, will you look at these papers? I think they're important."

His hand shook with the effort of his decision, as he held the papers out to Paulding. If the wind had just blown them away, he thought, he wouldn't have known anything about the plot. And how did he know it was a plot, anyway? He began to think he was being a fool again—as he felt so often.

The Skinner in the Hessian coat was shuffling through the papers. He looked sharply at the man on the ground, and then through the papers again. Then he said to his companions, "There ain't going to be no money in this business any way you figure it. We're going to turn him in to the American headquarters at North Castle."

"You think that's a good idea?" Van Wart said

"Sure I do. He's got papers on him about West Point. Mebbe somebody in the American army will give us a reward. We ain't going to let him go free."

"But that's ten miles!" Williams protested.

"No headquarters closer." Paulding was stubborn. "You can stay here if you want to, but the ones that takes him in are the ones gets the reward."

They considered the question solemnly. And then for the reward of what he had with him—his horse, saddle, watch, and jewelry—they decided to take him to North Castle. Jock was both sorry and relieved.

An hour later they arrived at the American post at North Castle, where Lieutenant Colonel John Jameson was in command. The orderly took their message, looking scornful of these ragged militia men. On the other side of the big, polished door, Colonel Jameson sounded querulous.

"What do the militiamen want?"

"They have a captive, sir, carrying suspicious papers."

"Very well," he said, in a resigned tone, "send them all in."

The party of seven Skinners trooped into the Colonel's office, surrounding John Anderson.

"John Anderson!" The Colonel recognized the name. He rose and shook hands with the prisoner and nodded to the Skinners. "We've got orders to look for this man," he said cheerfully. "You did well to bring him in. General Arnold wants to see him."

Relief rushed through Jock. He liked John Anderson —or Major André, whichever his name really was. Perhaps he *was* on official business for General Arnold.

"Sir," Paulding said, stepping forward, pulling nervously at his forelock, "we found these papers in the prisoner's boots, sir. Mebbe you ought to look at them."

Jameson glanced through the papers carelessly. "Oh, yes, of course. Well, I'm sure there will be an explanation for the papers. You can leave the business safely in our hands now." He looked down at the papers again.

"Sir . . ." Van Wart spoke up for his rights. "We're militiamen, sir, and the law lets us supplement the pay they gives us, and anyone knows it ain't much, for serving our country and all . . ." He ran out of breath and thoughts at the same time, and Paulding picked up what he was trying to say.

"Us militiamen are entitled to a prize when we bring in a prisoner like this, sir."

Colonel Jameson was considering the papers with some attention now, and he looked up as if he were recalled from concentration.

"Oh, yes. Prize. Of course. Suppose you take the prisoner's horse and trappings—would that be enough?"

He went back to the papers.

"Sir," Jock said, "may I ask for something that was taken from me, instead of the prize?"

By this time, Colonel Jameson had paled, and he looked at the ragged group before him as if seeing them for the first time.

"I think you deserve quite a bit for bringing in this man," he said, in a different tone.

"Now, young man," he said to Jock, "what was taken from you?"

"Someone took a rifle, sir. It wasn't mine. I mean, I borrowed it, and I must return it."

"Where is it now?"

"An innkeeper took it, the last I heard."

The Colonel looked at Van Wart. "Do you know anything of this?"

Van Wart grinned sheepishly. "I guess I forgot about it when we found this Anderson, Colonel. We're going over to the tavern now."

The Colonel looked stern. "When you recover this boy's rifle, bring it back here so I know he's got it. Then you can claim your prize. Is that understood?"

"Right enough." Van Wart saluted in the haphazard way the militia used, to indicate understanding. "Might as well take care of this little job right now, boys. Ain't nobody going to keep my prize from me, you bet!"

Chapter 16

THE party of seven men set out again, riding single file where the lanes were narrow, and bunched together when the road opened up. They were talking about how much money this captive was worth, and they argued about what they had lost in turning him in to the Americans. The British would have paid ransom for him, they were now sure.

Jock kept remembering that sunny day when Major André had sketched pretty Peggy Fraser, and he had spoken of another Peggy—Peggy Arnold. General Arnold. His hero. He recalled the General's glittering eyes. He had smiled at Jock, but his eyes had been cold . . .

Jock swerved away from that thought and deliberately recalled the purpose of this ride. Even with Colonel Jameson's orders, he would not feel sure of the Ferguson rifle until he held it in his hands again . . . And to think he might have taken home gold guineas for André's ransom, enough to buy his father out of jail . . . But André was carrying those papers that would have betrayed West Point to the British . . .

The argument with himself had come back to the

beginning of the circle, and Jock was sick with dread. Something disastrous overhung them all.

"What's the matter, kid?" one of his companions asked curiously. "You disappointed about the money, too?"

Jock shook his head. "Not the money. No."

"What's the trouble, then?"

"I just hope I get my gun back again."

"What's so great about this gun?" Williams asked curiously. "All I been hearing about is getting your gun back for you. How'd you lose it, anyway? Sounds kind of stupid to me."

Jock hunched his shoulders, not caring to argue about being stupid.

"Belongs to a friend of mine," he muttered. "I borrowed it. Can't go home without it."

"Doesn't pay to borrow another man's gun." One of the men began a long tedious anecdote about how the same thing had happened to him once. Jock hoped they had forgotten about his gun for awhile. Then he had an idea.

"If I get my rifle back again," he said to Williams, when the other man had finished his story, "I don't care about any of the prize for this—Anderson. You can divide up my share."

"Sure enough," Williams said jovially. "You mean, getting this gun is worth your share of the prize? Hey men!" He wheeled about and yelled to his comrades.

"The kid says we can split his share of the prize if we get his gun!"

"Yeah!" They raised their guns in salute, and Jock felt a little better. He hoped none of these good friends would decide to hold on to the Ferguson when he saw it.

The seven ragged men approached the tavernkeeper with coarse jests and rowdy jokes. They were feeling very important by now, because of the capture they had made. Jock tried to be as inconspicuous as possible, looking anxiously behind the bar to see if his gun was in sight, and relieved that there was no one else in the place. His companions ordered ale and stood at the bar while Mead filled their orders and watched warily for trouble. He was a ruddy-faced man with black hair and a suspicious expression.

"Mr. Mead," Van Wart said, "our friend here has lost a rifle gun, and last we heard you had it."

The tavernkeeper stopped, put both hands on the counter, and looked hostilely from one to another of his customers.

"Why would I have his gun? What kind of talk is this?"

Van Wart pulled Jock over to the bar to face Mead.

"Tell the man about your rifle gun, Jock."

Jock gulped, afraid of saying the wrong thing and getting Mr. Mead so annoyed with him that he might lose the gun for good, and terrified by the thought that perhaps it wasn't here after all.

"Mr. Mead, Mr. Mogan borrowed it. Now he says your

place was the last place he remembered being at, and he didn't have the gun when he went home."

Mead muttered something under his breath about too many Skinners buying drinks and then not having anything to pay for them with.

Van Wart slapped a heavy hand on the bar. "What did he owe, Mead?"

"How would I know? What night was it?"

"Two nights ago."

Mead grumbled something about not knowing anything about the gun. Van Wart said, "Mr. Mead, where is it? Hand it over, or we'll take the place apart."

Van Wart's companions had crowded behind him and alongside, muskets in hand, bayonets bristling. There was no one else in the tavern.

"You ain't got no call to be raiding me," Mead whined, angry and frightened. "I'm as good a Patriot as anyone around here!"

"All we want is the kid's gun, Mead."

Van Wart tramped around behind the bar, and the tavernkeeper backed against the wall. "Get outa here! Get out!" he yelled.

"Aw, shut your mouth!" Van Wart flung some pewter mugs to the brick floor. "What's under the counter?"

"Here! Wait! Stop a minute! I'll get the gun! You don't need to pull the place down!"

Mead ran with heavy shuffling steps into a back room and ran out again with the Ferguson in his hand, just as

Van Wart was pouring himself a drink from a bottle. He flung the empty bottle on the floor where it shattered on the bricks.

"Is this the gun you're talking about?"

Jock reached over and clutched the Ferguson. "That's it! Mr. Mead, I'm sure glad to get it back again!"

"Don't thank me!" Mead growled. "Just take your friends away and don't come back."

"Mr. Van Wart . . ." Jock nudged him. "Shall we ride back and get that prize?"

With joyful whoops the party set out again. Jock thought wistfully of leaving them at the first fork in the road, and going on home. But the Colonel had said they could have the prize loot only when he saw that the gun was in Jock's hands.

For a minute, there at headquarters, Jock was afraid the American officers were going to keep the gun. They liked the feeling of it, they passed it among themselves, talking about how easy it would be to win a war, if you had enough rifle guns like that. Then Colonel Jameson handed it back to Jock.

"Take good care of that firing piece, boy. It's the best rifle gun I've ever seen. I wouldn't want it to get into British hands. Where did you get it, anyway?"

"From a British deserter!"

The officers laughed at that, and the Colonel distributed the loot: the gold watch, horse, saddle, and bridle.

"How are you men going to divide it up?"

The American officers passed the gun around

While the Skinners argued about their spoils, Jock slipped away and started home. It seemed as if he'd been gone forever.

Maggie and Peggy threw themselves upon him. His mother hugged him tight, and then suddenly released him. "Jock! Where have you been all this time? I was afraid they got you like your pa."

"Hasn't anyone found Pa yet?"

His mother shook her head, and tears sprang to her eyes. "The neighbors been asking around. But Cartwright's taken so many now, everyone's a-feared. Didn't the Skinners—I thought you were going out with them to find him!" She looked at him accusingly.

"We tried Cartwright's place, but he had a crowd of guards at the jail—and Pa might not be there. He may be in New York—nobody knows."

She wrung her hands. "What will we do next?"

"Is Dick here?"

"Dick's here," she said bitterly. "I'm sure I don't know why he's here when your pa's gone."

Jock went out to the forge, the Ferguson swinging at his side. Dick was bending over the work table, dismantling an old gun. At the sound of Jock's step he swung around suddenly, as if he were on guard.

"Oh, it's you," he said.

"I brought your Ferguson rifle gun back. I grabbed it when I went out to find Pa because—well, because it's

156

so much better than any other gun around the place."

Dick nodded. He took the gun, looked it over, cocked and pulled the trigger. "Well," he said at last, "I'm glad it's back."

He looked tired and a little haggard, as if something were troubling him, more important than the return of the Ferguson.

"When I heard the yells last Thursday I thought they got you along with Pa," Jock said.

Dick looked at him sideways, and then dropped his eyes, fiddling with the sharp tool he had been using, picking at the surface of the work table.

"When they grabbed your pa, I—well—I got away." He looked up, beyond Jock, out of the open door. "I didn't dare get taken, being a deserter. I didn't dare! You understand that?" He stared at Jock with a haggard look. "They woulda run me back to the British army. I woulda been flogged—and hanged . . ." His head dropped. "All I did was get away. And I been feeling terrible ever since."

Jock remembered how frightened he had been with the Skinners on Thursday night, when a comrade was shot. He would have run then, if he could. And somehow he liked Dick better than he ever had.

"Tell me what happened, Dick."

Dick talked fast, as if he were glad to be unburdening himself.

"I never could tell your ma, Jock, and every time she

looked at me she was wondering why I was there and your pa was gone. But this mounted patrol came along and stopped at the forge. Your pa thought they wanted guns repaired, and he said, 'Good evening, gentlemen, how can I serve you?' The leader says, 'I've got a warrant for your arrest, Fraser. Non-payment of rent.' And your pa said 'So?' as if he'd been expecting it some time. Then the leader says, 'The squire says if you come along quietly and work for him the duration of the war he'll consider the rent paid, free and clear.' Your pa says, 'I don't work for that Tory.' And then they tell him, 'If you send your boy to help with the iron works, you can have iron for gun barrels, and forget the rent, too.' And at that your pa yells, 'Get out of my forge, you so and so Tories!' "

"That's what I heard," Jock said. "I ran out, fast as I could pick up a gun, and he was already gone. And so were you."

"When I heard them talking about working on guns for Cartwright," Dick said somberly, "that's when I knew I better get out of the way. I got around back of the forge while they were talking. And I was trying to load a gun—but there weren't any bullets to fit the one I picked up." He dropped his head in his hands. "They grabbed him, tied him up, and slung him across a saddle before I could find another gun, and then they were gone. If I'd just had the Ferguson I coulda stood them off. But you know how your pa was about that gun—

always fearful someone would raid the forge and steal it . . ."

"We rode up to Cartwright's jail that night," Jock said. "We couldn't force it—they had twenty men on guard. And I didn't have the Ferguson with me, either!"

He told Dick what had happened, and both smiled a little bitterly. Dick said, "But I shoulda done *something*. I don't know what it coulda been. But something. Peggy seemed to understand how it was . . ." He jumped up and paced back and forth in the smithy. "There's been something going on—people coming and going, neighbors talking about something in the air. I didn't think the women should be left alone."

Jock recalled the feeling he had had, the weeks before his father was taken, that something was going to happen in the valley. And then he remembered the Skinners' captive of that very morning.

"We picked up a British officer this morning," he said. It seemed like days ago, now. "He was carrying papers about West Point."

"Who was it?"

"Major André."

"André!" Dick cried. "He was head of intelligence for the British in the Hudson Valley!"

Jock described the capture. "I think I coulda got him off," he said. "I was the only one could read the papers, besides Paulding. But in the end I knew Pa would rather stay in jail than be bought out with British gold . . ."

Dick stood up, tall, as if he had reached a decision. He picked up the Ferguson again and hefted it lovingly.

"Now that you're home again, I can leave," he said. "I'm going out and find where your pa is."

He went back to the house with Jock, where they collected a pouch of bullets for the Ferguson, a blanket, a packet of food.

"I think Dick is wonderful," Peggy announced, leaning out of the window and watching him till he turned the bend in the road.

"Aw, you think all the British are wonderful," Jock told her.

"But Dick isn't British any more," she announced. "He's really going to be an American when this war is over."

Chapter 17

ON SUNDAY morning, Maggie Fraser made blueberry pancakes. Eating them, Jock felt as if yesterday's nightmare had blown away with the night. But his mother just picked at her food, eating hardly anything. Once she said, "I wonder if your pa is getting anything to eat. They don't feed prisoners much . . ."

"Jock!" Peggy pulled him outside the door after breakfast. "Do you think Dick can find Pa?"

"I think Pa's in Cartwright's jail, right back of his house," Jock said. "If he isn't there, Dick's going to New York and hunt around. And that's pretty brave of him, when he might be picked up for a deserter."

"When will we know?"

Jock looked at his sister. Could he trust her?

"I could have brought home enough gold guineas to make us rich yesterday," he told her. "It's been worrying me all along that I could have got Pa outa jail and didn't . . ."

"Jock, why didn't you?" she wailed.

He stared at the ground, recalling that hard decision.

"We picked up a spy yesterday morning," he said. "He offered us ten thousand guineas in gold to let him go."

"But why didn't you take it?" she breathed. "Jock! Think what it would have meant to Pa!"

"I've been thinking about it," he said grimly. "The spy was carrying papers that would have betrayed West Point to the British. You think Pa would rather lose the war than stay in jail? I couldn't take that money."

"West Point! To give it to the British!" She looked as dazed as Jock had felt, and he wondered again if it really had been true.

"When Dick gets back I want to go up to West Point and see Rob," he said. "Maybe I can find out about the papers. Maybe there was some mistake."

"You can tell him about Pa," Peggy said practically. "I think Ma would feel better if she thought Rob knew." Then, "Who was the spy?"

Jock looked at her, to make his announcement more important. "It was Major André of the British army. Remember when he stopped with us that day?"

"Jock! It couldn't have been!"

He shrugged. "That's what everyone thought. He said his name was John Anderson. And that was what his pass said—and the pass was signed by General Arnold. But I knew it was Major André."

"Oh!" She was light-hearted again. "The whole thing is a monstrous mistake. How silly to worry about a thing like that!"

Of course. How silly to worry. He wondered why he couldn't seem to stop worrying.

A horseman was approaching from far down the road, and Peggy turned like a bird dog. "Maybe that's Dick!"

They ran toward the road, and Peggy reached it first. Jock was irritated because his sister could run faster than he could—and she was younger! But the horseman was indeed Dick, and Jock forgot his annoyance as they accompanied him to the stable, and listened to his story, while he rubbed down his horse.

"I found your pa. They weren't guarding him so close this morning, right after dawn. He's in the guardhouse back of Cartwright's place, and when the guard went off to the kitchen I crawled up behind the place and called, and your pa answered me."

"How can we get him out of there?" Jock demanded.

Dick rubbed down the mare's pastern with great attention.

"He says you're not to come near the place, not on any account. If Cartwright gets hold of you, your pa says, he'll hide you where no one can find you—like in New York. He's getting desperate for gunsmiths . . . Your pa says he'd rot in jail before he'd let you work for the man."

"But you're a better gunsmith than I am," Jock cried. "Why didn't he kidnap you, while you were on his ground?"

Dick grinned. "He don't know me. Not yet. Nor his guards don't know me. I rode in like a Loyalist spy for Major André. I let them think I was part of his intelligence service, on my way up to Peekskill to spy on General Washington. They know some way that Washington is going through Peekskill on his way to West Point. Up there on the plantation they think the war is going to be over in a couple of days."

"Do they know about Major André being captured?"

"I was just listening," Dick said. "I wasn't talking. Nobody mentioned André."

"The country's full of spies," Jock said broodingly. "There could be spies in West Point itself." There must be others than Arnold, he told himself with desperate hope. "Someone stole those papers and forged Arnold's signature. . ."

But even as he found this plausible explanation, the sense of doom seemed closer and darker than ever. Something was going to happen, and he felt that nothing could prevent it. He left Peggy talking to Dick and walked back to the house to tell his mother what Dick had found out.

"Ma, I'm going to ride up to West Point tomorrow morning and talk with Rob about Pa."

She smiled at him, looking more cheerful than at any time since he'd come home. "You do that, Jock. I'd feel much better if Rob knew about it."

Early Monday morning Jock rode up the road toward West Point. He planned to ride up the east bank and make the crossing at Anthony's Nose. But when he reached the crossing point, soon after eight, the ferry seemed to be waiting on the other side, below Fort Montgomery. He slid off his horse, tethered her to a maple tree, and sat down on a rock overlooking the river, to wait.

Now that he was on his way to West Point, he felt more composed than at any time during the past several days. In the morning freshness he was sure there was a foolish mistake in his fears about General Arnold. He thought back over the General's heroic record, and became more reassured as he recalled it.

Benedict Arnold had taken Fort Schuyler, back in '77, when his own General Schuyler had said it couldn't be done. He had captured vast stores of ammunition for the American army. And Patriots had chuckled for days over the ingenious ruse he had used. . . . He had led an assault at Freeman's farm, and the British General Burgoyne had said, "Only that attack saved the Americans from absolute defeat." . . . He had fought at Bemis Heights with such fury that he led the men to superhuman efforts to carry the day. And that battle had been responsible for the surrender of Burgoyne's whole army, at Saratoga. Why, he had been a greater general and greater Patriot than half a dozen of Washington's other generals put together!

The warm autumn sunlight was striking golden tones from the bronze and scarlet foliage, and he began to feel good again.

It was nine o'clock now, and across the river the soldiers were moving back and forth at Fort Montgomery. The ferry should be crossing any time now. The sun lit the rocky black-forested western bank of the Hudson, and overhead an eagle hovered, poised to strike some helpless prey hidden in the forest below. Jock watched him idly. The bird was plunging now, claws outstretched. As he disappeared into the trees, a hurried splashing caught the boy's ear.

A couple of miles upstream, near West Point, a barge was heading downstream in full sail. He watched it come, admiring the speed it was making. He could count six pairs of oars, rising and falling with swift precision. With the wind behind it, the sails stood out firm and hard.

The barge approached Anthony's Nose with urgency in the very rhythm of the oars. Jock stared intently as it passed. And then he sprang to his feet. Sitting upright, arms folded, eyes staring hard ahead, was General Benedict Arnold. And pulling the third oar in the boat was Rob Fraser.

Jock yelled and waved. But the crew was too intent on pulling at maximum speed to hear anything from the bank. The barge was running down the middle of the river, avoiding the shorelines and, while Jock watched, it sped around the bend of Anthony's Nose and out of sight.

He ran back to the mare, unfastened the reins, and

leaped into the saddle. If Rob was running downstream with Arnold, there was no reason for Jock to go on to West Point. He turned back to the path along the river and followed the barge.

Sometimes he feared he might not catch her: she was taking a course as nearly straight as possible, and Jock's road wound in and out along a rugged shoreline. Even when he could gallop the horse, she could hardly make more time than the barge running with the current and the wind behind new sails.

There were miles where he was away from the river bank, and he was afraid he might have missed the spot where she might be heading. But as he crossed the Peekskill, she was flying toward King's Ferry. And as he passed King's Ferry, the barge was running into Haverstraw Bay. She passed Slaughter's Landing at the same speed and came into the Tappan Sea. And there the *Vulture* stood at anchor.

Jock was opposite the barge now, and he rode along the shoreline watching her every move. As she approached the *Vulture,* the oars slackened their speed. She came alongside, and one of the oarsmen reached up and tied the barge in position. General Arnold spoke to the oarsmen and scrambled up the rope ladder. His lame leg made him clumsy. The oarsmen followed him aboard.

Jock slid off his horse, tethered her, and sat down to watch the sloop. General Arnold had been so ingenious in plotting to deceive the British when he took Fort

Schuyler that the Hudson Valley had resounded with laughter from Ticonderoga to Dobbs Ferry. Probably he had a plot now that must be presented to British officers aboard the *Vulture,* something that would sweep the British out of the Hudson and out of New York when they acted upon it.

While he watched, one of the *Vulture's* small boats put off for the eastern shore. It landed almost below where Jock was sitting, and a man climbed out and up the bluff. He was wearing an American uniform, and at the top he stopped a moment, shook his fist at the *Vulture,* and then turned into the road going north. Jock moved out and intercepted him.

"Sir! You just came from the *Vulture?"*

"What's it to you?" the man snarled. A string of oaths ripped from his lips, and suddenly he broke down, sobbing with fury. "That Arnold!" he cried. "I told myself, climbing up that bluff, it ain't true! He didn't do it! And then I remember he did. And it's like to kill the men!"

"What happened?" Jock cried, feeling his knees begin to shake. "My brother was in that boat. Rob Fraser."

"Aye! Rob Fraser. One of the men from the garrison. He took the place this morning for Willy, who got sick in the night. The General always wanted his barge awaiting at the shore to take him to the Point after breakfast. Some days we waited till noon before he's ready to go. But this morning . . ." He swiped the angry tears from

Jock moved out and intercepted him

his eyes with a dirty paw, and his mouth hardened. ". . . This morning he comes running down the bank about nine o'clock and says, 'Take me to the *Vulture,* men, fast as you can. Urgent business with the officer there.'"

Jock felt his throat drying, and he thought he was going to be sick. "But—why did the men go aboard?"

"He telled us we'd get two gallons of rum, if we got him there quick. And we was quick. He complimented us, even, what fine oarsmen we were. And we was thirsty —running nigh onto twenty miles at top speed like that. So we went aboad. And *then* he says"—he mimicked the General's official tones with terrible bitterness—"he says to me, 'I regret to have to tell you, Mr. Coxswain, but you and your men must consider yourselves prisoners of Captain Sutherland!' I near to bounced him off the ship right then. But there was Captain Sutherland and half the British navy staring me in the eye, and I refrained." His voice was scaldingly ironic.

"What's happening to the men now?" Jock cleared his throat.

"I telled Captain Sutherland we wasn't prepared for prison, having no clothes and no warning, so to speak. General Arnold keeps saying, 'I must be in New York as quick as possible, Captain.' But the Captain don't like this traitor no more than the rest of us, and he says, cool as you please, 'Coxswain, I'll take your parole and you may go ashore and find clothes for your men. We'll wait for you here.' And you can bet I'm in no hurry."

"My horse is over here." Jock turned toward the spot where the mare was tethered. "She can carry us both, and I'll help you collect Rob's things." He gulped, feeling as if he were helping prepare for Rob's funeral. The coxswain nodded.

"I'll be glad to ride. There's a many miles to go, finding food and clothes for them six men." He smiled sardonically. "I don't mind dragging my feet. I figure every minute he waits, Arnold is going to sweat."

As they rode, he recovered his composure, and his anger turned into melancholy. He figured the best thing would be to ride up to headquarters at North Castle and collect what supplies might be found there.

"Ma will send some food back to the men," Jock told him. "She made a couple of meat pasties just yesterday."

The coxswain brightened considerably. "I'm kinda hungry myself," he said. "What with tearing down that river so early in the morning. It was upsetting, that's what it was, taking him to that ship."

"But *why* did he do it?" Jock cried again.

The coxswain shook his head bitterly. "You mark my words, there's money in it for him. He got paid . . ."

By late afternoon he had had a good meal at the Frasers, and repeated for Mrs. Fraser and Peggy the story he had told Jock earlier. He added, "I wouldn't be surprised,

Ma'am, if the captain let the men go. He was disgusted hisself, and he a British officer, that an American officer could turn in his own men that way. Only reason I'm going back is my parole. If I broke that the rest of the men might never get out."

Jock took a second horse for the trip back to the spot opposite the *Vulture,* and helped the coxswain down the bank with the bundles of food and clothing.

"Watch out for Rob for us!" he said, as the coxswain signaled the boat that he was ready to return. Then, as the boat left the *Vulture,* Jock cried, "Come back when the war's over," and climbed up the bluff and hid in the undergrowth before the boat could reach the shore. There he waited to see the *Vulture* leave, hopeful that, as the coxswain had suggested, the other oarsmen might be set free.

Night had fallen, and he strained his eyes to see the ship. She raised anchor and set sail downstream for New York.

And Jock, watching her go, with General Arnold and his bargemen aboard, knew now there was no other answer at all: a Patriot general had tried to betray his country. He had tried to sell West Point—for money.

Chapter 18

Jock woke at cockscrow on Tuesday morning, feeling as if he were black and blue all over. For a moment he could not think why he should be so tired. The early morning air was chill and fresh, and the down quilt lusciously warm. He snuggled under it and shut his eyes, feeling as if there were something out there he didn't want to face. The cocks crowed again.

"Jock? You up?" His mother was calling. "There's much to do today."

Reluctantly he crawled out of the warm bed and set his bare feet on the painted floor. It was icy, and he waked suddenly. And then he remembered: Benedict Arnold had gone over to the British. And he had delivered Rob as a prisoner. The tired, numb feeling came back.

When he got down to the warm kitchen, Peggy was already out in the chilly morning milking the cow. Jock fetched pails of water, brought in armloads of wood for the fire, carried in the heavy pans of clotted cream for churning. Maggie Fraser was moving about with quick steps, mixing bread and setting it to rise before breakfast. By the time breakfast was ready at eight o'clock, Jock was hungry enough to eat a bear.

"All I can think of is your poor pa, over in Cartwright's jail. Cold as winter—and not knowing whether he's getting a bite to eat, or a blanket to keep him warm."

One of the men down the road came by to tell Mrs. Fraser the news about Arnold.

"I know," she said. "My boy Rob was one of his boatmen, and the craven liar turned him in for a prisoner."

"Arnold will hang for sure," the neighbor prophesied hopefully.

"Aye—and will my son come home?"

He went on to carry the news further, and a man rode up with a newspaper from Peekskill.

"They caught Major André, and General Arnold escaped," he announced.

"And it's a dirty shame it wasn't the other way around!" Maggie Fraser snapped. "Betraying his own men like that."

"It's more than the boatmen he wanted to betray," the man said grimly. "He woulda sold the whole country back to the king, if he'd had his way."

"Hanging's too good for him!"

"So it is. But they'll have to catch him first."

He rode on and Jock finished his breakfast in gulps.

A traveler came by and asked for breakfast and repeated the news. The valley was ringing with it now, and Jock wondered aloud how old man Cartwright would be taking it.

"If he knew what was good for him, he'd turn loose his

prisoners," Maggie said. "Tories aren't going to be very popular around here, after yesterday's work."

It was time to get out to the forge, and Jock and Dick went out to await any work that might come in. Half an hour later one of the soldiers from West Point rode up and stacked half a dozen muskets against the wall. "Can these be mended right away? General Washington wants all the equipment in fighting shape."

"What's going to happen up there?" Jock asked, taking apart the gunlock on the first gun.

The man scowled. "We're finally repairing the walls," he said. "They been needing that all this summer. New commandant is coming in tomorrow. We'll be all right, I guess."

"Why would Arnold turn on us like that?" Jock cried. "After Saratoga and all . . . ?"

"Money," said the man harshly. "You hear it around the Point all the time. He'd do anything for money—sell his country, sell his soul."

He went away again, and Jock bent over the rusted gunlock. He might have taken the British gold for André's freedom, and he hadn't chosen money. He wondered now about that. Pa could have taken Cartwright's money, in exchange for his own freedom . . . Money bought a lot of things, indeed.

By five o'clock the guns were repaired, polished, oiled and ready. Jock looked at them with the bitter cynicism that had made him unhappy for three days now. What difference did it make how many Americans had fighting equipment, if their top officers were trying to sell them to the enemy?

The man from the garrison came to pick up the guns, and handed Jock Continental bills.

"My pa wants silver," Jock said scornfully, rejecting the bills.

"This is the money of the country I'm fighting for," the soldier snapped. "This is the pay I gotta take home. Who do you think you are?"

He threw the Continental paper on the floor and stalked out with the guns across his back. Dick began to clean up the forge. Jock watched Dick pick up the bills and put them away. Dick scattered the coals in the forge to cool, closed the shutters, replaced the tools, swept the floor. Jock turned his back and went up to the house, as one of the Skinners rode up to the door.

"We're going to run the Tories out of this valley tonight," he told Jock. "Report to my house soon's you can. We figure it's time to get rid of them after Arnold's dirty treason."

For the first time that day Jock felt a stirring of hope. "Cartwright?" he asked.

"Him first of all. Don't let it out, but we been talking to some of his men, and they won't try to stop us."

When Jock met them, forty Skinners had collected. He looked around for Van Wart, hoping to avoid him.

"He went with the crowd meeting at Taylor's place,"

one of the men said. "We're hitting the Tories in as many places as we can tonight. We figure Arnold couldn't have got so far with his monkey business without some help from the Tories. We're going to get rid of all the Redcoat lovers around here, and old man Cartwright is going to be the first."

Jock rode soberly along near the front of the line of riders. He wanted to get his father out of Cartwright's jail. But he couldn't hate all Tories, the way these Skinners did. Ahead of him the torches flared meancingly, and he could hear shouts about tar and feathers.

The cool autumn night closed in. The crickets made a bickering undertone, a hoot owl called, and once he saw the eyes of a raccoon shining in the torchlight. The line of night-riders crossed the bridge over the Croton, and pounded into the plantation. Tonight it was unnecessary to be quiet.

"The old Tory don't know it," one of the men bragged, riding alongside Jock, "but plenty of his own men will be glad to sell him out."

Something in that phrase rang unpleasantly for Jock. Sell him out—men who had been willing to work for him and take his money. At least Pa wouldn't work for a man he hated. A new sense of pride in Pa was forming, for Jock. Money had never been able to buy him. Surprisingly, the thought that Cartwright's own men would be willing to betray him aroused a kind of pity for the man that Jock had never expected to feel.

The sound of pounding hoofs was approaching the Skinners, and with a sudden caution, the whole line moved from the road to line up along the edge, their torches lighting the way. They sat motionless, grinning like wolves.

Six men rode by, rifles cocked. They were wearing Cartwright's livery, and ready to shoot at the first leaf that stirred. Behind them the big Cartwright coach thundered past, its torches streaming, the four matched horses pulling in unison at a gallop.

In the torchlight Jock saw one of the Cartwright girls shrinking back from the window, her hat askew, her eyes big with fright. Beside her, Oliver Cartwright was glaring from side to side, a cocked pistol glinting in his hand. The coachman was urging the horses to top speed, and the man at his side held his rifle at the ready. Behind the coach six more outriders rode armed. But the cortege was more concerned with flight than with battle, and while the Skinners stood motionless, they fled past without a shot.

The Skinners watched the coach roll past, laughing. A couple of them yelled oaths and ugly threats. But none moved to stop it.

"So long as he's on his way to New York, let him go! He's left a lot behind! Hey, men! On to the plantation."

Some of the men rode up to the beautiful front door and battered at it with gun butts. Two who were impatient with the heavy door smashed the bowed window of

The Cartwright coach thundered past

the front room out of its frame and stepped through. Jock made straight for the jailhouse, and found himself alone.

"Pa! Hey, Pa! We've come to get you out!"

"I'm still here."

Pa's voice sounded kind of weak, and Jock quailed. He began battering on the door with his musket. Then he rushed off again, to find a sledgehammer and crowbar. His Skinner friends were too concerned with looting the beautiful house to care about anything else.

When the door was finally down, Jock found his father sitting on the dirt floor.

"You all right, Pa?" Jock leaned over him.

"Kinda tired of sitting here in the dark." George Fraser sounded like his old sardonic self. Jock helped him to his feet and tucked his arm under his father's arm, shocked that he seemed weak and unsteady.

But his father joked about it. "I'm used to more food than I got in there," he said, with a bitter little chuckle.

Jock got his father on his horse and led him to the big house, where, he figured, there should be some food left in the kitchen quarters. The slaves were watching, with big, frightened eyes, the ruffians who were looking into every cupboard, picking up the silver, spitting on the floor. Jock had known the cook from earlier days.

"Cassie, my pa has been starving out there in the jailhouse. Got anything to eat before I take him home?"

Cassie was so relieved to see someone she knew that

she grinned all across her face. "I shore have, Jock. Just set you both down and let me bring it on. They were eating my fried chicken tonight when the alarm came, and Mr. Cartwright, he couldn't finish his supper he was so scared . . ."

"We'll finish it for him."

Halfway through his meal George Fraser looked up. "Cassie, I hate to say so, but that was worth a week in jail. It's even better than Maggie's fried chicken."

The old brick kitchen was warm and friendly in the candlelight and firelight. Jock sat back and watched his pa eat. In the house he could hear smashing and screeching. It made him kind of sick to have such a beautiful house torn apart. But there was something else he should take care of, while he was here, and he was trying to think what it was.

"What are you going to do now, Cassie?" he asked.

"Guess we'll just stay on and try to keep the place going somehow," she said.

And then Jock remembered. "Cassie, where's the forge-master? Is he going to run with the others?"

"He's gone back to the village tonight," she said. "But he say he going to keep the furnace running, long as the men bring iron out of the hills. They all got to live, Jock. And Mr. Peasely say he can make a good living making iron, whether Mr. Cartwright here or gone."

"I reckon maybe the British can't buy his iron any more, with the valley feeling the way it does now," he said.

"Reckon not."

George Fraser looked up. He had been listening silently while he finished the fried chicken, and now he was ready to talk.

"Cassie, you tell Mr. Peasely I'll ride up tomorrow and talk to him about iron. I'll be wanting as much as I can get."

"I'll tell him, Mr. Fraser."

"You tell him this, Cassie. The Americans are going to win this war. Mr. Cartwright isn't going to be back, and I'm going to be around a long, long time—making guns."

She laughed richly. "I'll sure tell him, Mr. Fraser. That Mr. Peasely, he's going to be glad to sell you iron. He just as soon see the Americans win this war!"

Chapter 19

O N THURSDAY morning the first load of iron came
down from the plantation and Fraser Forge began
making muskets for the American army again.

"Mebbe I was wrong about taking only silver money,"
George Fraser conceded, when he was figuring the cost
of the new muskets. "I guess Washington has enough
troubles without us giving him money trouble besides.
We're all in this together, and we'll get out together."

The sun was going down Thursday night when they
heard the women shrieking in the house. Jock set out on
a run. George Fraser and Dick followed on his heels.
They burst into the kitchen, muskets in hand.

There stood Rob, laughing at all of them, while Maggie was crying with happiness and Peggy was laughing
and crying at the same time.

"Rob! I thought you were in a British prison for the
rest of the war!" Jock pounded his brother on the back.

"I thought so too, when we got on the *Vulture*," Rob
said. "Coxswain told me he saw my family, so I knew
you heard about it—our own general giving us in to the
British like that."

"But what happened to Arnold?" Jock cried.

Rob shook his head in disgust and stuffed a piece of bread in his mouth. "I haven't had much to eat since we got to New York," he said, chewing it with relish. "We got there Tuesday night, and Wednesday morning Arnold marches us all to Clinton's headquarters and tells him he's reporting for command with the British army and brought seven prisoners with him. General Clinton looks at us and says, "Are you men deserting?" and coxswain says, 'No, sir. Our general here told us to consider ourselves prisoners, and so we do. Against our will!' Clinton looked disgusted, I swear. And he says, 'General Arnold I fear this is an unnecessary meanness.' And then he says, 'Men, I'll take your parole not to fight again, and you can go home.'"

"Parole not to fight!" Maggie Fraser cried, ruffling up like an angry little hen.

"That's right, Ma. I'm home to stay."

"I must say, I don't like the idea of any British general telling my son he can't fight for Washington if he wants to!"

Jock laughed in spite of himself. Ma had complained so long and tearfully about Rob being in the army. And now she was mad because he was going to be out of the army.

"There's nothing funny about it!" She snapped at Jock. "We're fighting to be free of British rule, and if Rob is free he can fight if he wants to, and I won't hold him back."

"But a parole is a word of honor," Rob explained patiently. "Either I give my parole and wait out the war at home, or I refuse to give it and wait it out in a British prison. Either way I don't fight."

"But now that you're home, I think you can fight if you want to," she insisted.

"You don't break your parole like that, Ma. It's a matter of honor."

"A lot of honor Clinton had, when he was buying out one of our generals," she sniffed.

Rob gave up, smiling at Jock as if to say "You can't explain a matter of honor to women, they don't understand it the way we men do." But Jock turned away. The dark conviction swept over him again that there was no longer any honor in the world.

"What really happened with Arnold last week?" George Fraser wanted to know.

"We don't know the bottom of it yet," Rob said. "The boatmen were dumbfounded when he turned us in to the captain of the *Vulture*." He shook his head. "We talked among ourselves on the run down to New York. We could see then all the little things fitting together—like sending so many of the garrison to cut wood and make a guard at Fishkill. If the British had attacked, we would have been undermanned any time after he took command."

"What did he do about the chain there?" his father demanded.

"He never did anything. The chain was sinking, the logs were water-soaked. A heavy-loaded vessel could have broken it."

George Fraser nodded with the pleasure of a man who has known it all along. "Some men will do anything for a dollar, and Arnold had the look stamped on his face. Now Major André, there, he was a gentleman. I remember the time he stopped here to get his pistol fixed. What's going to happen to him?"

"They don't know. Some of the men said Clinton is frantic for his fate. Loved him like a son."

Jock withdrew into gloom. He was beginning to wish he had saved André after all. British or not, John André was one man he still felt he could trust.

"Where are the Americans keeping him?" George Fraser asked.

"Nobody seems to know."

The next day, Friday, Rob joined the other men in the forge, and the work moved fast and smoothly. Jock worked harder than any of them. While he was working, he could forget about Arnold and André. He could forget about his own grief. But when the work was done, and he was lying sleepless in the dark, watching the moon sink low outside his window, he hated the world.

On Saturday, the word reached the valley and was passed around from neighbor to neighbor that Major André was imprisoned at Tappan, and condemned to die on Monday at noon.

The cloud of uncertainty closed in again, and Jock found himself unable to fight it off. What about the new commandant of West Point? What about Lafayette, the other officers of the American army, George Washington himself? Which one of them would try to sell the country next? How could he ever again trust anyone?

"That fine young man," Maggie Fraser said sadly. "It's a sorrowful thing it couldn't have been Arnold instead."

Peggy said nothing. Tears filled her big blue eyes and rolled down her cheeks, and then, sniffling, she left the table and slammed the door of her bedroom behind her.

"Monday at noon, did they say?" George Fraser asked. "I'd like to pay my respects, in a case like this. Just to show how little we like our own traitor. I think we'll go down to Tappan on Monday."

Dressed in their best clothes, the Frasers set out early Monday morning in the farm wagon to drive the twelve miles down the river to Tappan.

"I don't know why I should care," Maggie Fraser was saying, as they came off the ferry on the west bank and started down the road. "But that young man made a fine impression the day he stopped with us. You remember that day? So gentlemanly, so polite and courteous."

Peggy nodded, her eyes still reddened from weeping. "He said he had known another Peggy—and now she's Peggy Arnold." She gulped and pulled out her handkerchief again.

After that there was very little conversation. Each of them rode with his own thoughts. Jock watched the parade of color on the highland hills, and tried not to think about the occasion before them.

They reached Tappan an hour before noon. An enormous crowd was milling quietly about a stone building with a painted sign swinging outside the door: Mabie's Tavern. The crowd drifted back of the tavern toward a hill beyond an open field. The Frasers found a place to leave the wagon, and they joined the crowd at the foot of the hill. Atop the hill stood the black frame of a gallows.

In the crowd Jock heard whispers and rumor and gossip. "They say he asked to be shot. But it looks like hanging." "Too bad it isn't Arnold." "I shouldn't be feeling so bad about an English spy. But I can't help grieving for Major André." "If Arnold had any sense of honor, he'd give himself up and save a man like André." Someone laughed bitterly at the thought of Arnold and honor.

The Frasers moved through the crowd, now and then recognizing a friend from their part of the valley. An American officer who stood nearby looked familiar, and then Jock recognized Captain McLane. He looked sad and stern.

As the drumroll sounded, The Frasers found themselves standing near the foot of the hill. A parade of American troops was approaching, with the slow step of the death march, to the gibbet, where they stood in formation.

The death-roll of the drums sounded again, and the crowd shifted slightly. Major André was approaching in full-dress uniform, walking between two American officers. Now and then he bowed to someone he knew, as if he was pleased to see him there. The crowd was intensely silent.

He stood waiting near the gallows, rolling a stone under his foot, back and forth. Looking at his face, Jock saw he was swallowing hard. A wagon was pulled up the hill directly beneath the rope hanging from the gallows. The back dropped to form a ramp, and in the wagon was a coffin. Jock felt a lump forming in his own throat and he had to swallow several times before he could get rid of it. He was holding himself so tight that he was shaking a little.

Major André walked up the sloping ramp into the wagon and stepped upon the coffin. He took off his hat and laid it to one side. He looked up at the high gibbet and seemed to shrink. But he straightened at once. "It will be but a momentary pang," he said aloud.

The executioner stepped beside him, his face disguised with blackened grease, and picked up the loop of rope. André pushed him away with a motion of disgust and took the halter himself, to put it about his neck. He pulled a clean handkerchief from his pocket and bandaged his own eyes.

"Major André," one of the American officers said to him, "is there any last word you wish to say?"

A wagon was pulled up directly beneath the rope

Raising the handkerchief from his eyes, André looked into the eyes of the crowd. He said clearly, "I pray you bear me witness that I die like a brave man."

A choking sob filled Jock's throat and he closed his eyes to hold back the tears. He heard the grating of the wagon wheels, and he shuddered. When he opened his eyes the British officer was swinging at the end of the rope.

"He died instantly," Rob said, laying his arm across Jock's shoulders. "He was brave, as he wished to be."

"But I could have saved him!" Jock muttered.

His father turned to him. "Jock, it was him or your country," he said firmly.

The quiet crowd was beginning to break up and move away. The Frasers walked slowly toward their wagon.

The dirt road had been beaten hard and smooth by pounding hoofs, and the wagon rolled along easily. The warm October sun struck brilliantly through the trees. Farmers were walking back to their fields, mothers were pushing broods of children out of the way of the horses, barefoot boys were scuffing through the dust saying nothing.

Along the range of hills the gold and scarlet colors of October draped the ranges like flaring banners. The scarlet reminded Jock of a gallant British officer . . . a patriotic and courageous man.

Author's Note

JOHN ANDRÉ, who died bravely, is still remembered for his gallantry and courage. Spying for one's country was dangerous and often a dirty occupation. But it required courage, loyalty, and sacrifice. André's loyalty has always been admired, and a monument to his heroism is in Westminster Abbey.

Arnold got the money he bargained for. But money was his first goal, and he never got enough. He died in debt. Nor did he ever gain the glory he expected from England. His change of sides brought only distrust and abuse from the people he went to.

Major André, Captain McLane, and Major Wayne were all in the Hudson River area at the time of the story, and their activities were all as described.

Benedict Arnold was given command of West Point on August 3, 1870. He plotted the delivery of that vital post with John André; the plot failed because Arnold sent André back to his own lines by land, out of uniform. Arnold escaped as described, because he was informed of André's capture.

The Neutral Ground and the Skinners and Cowboys are historical. Williams, Paulding, and Van Wart are named in original records of the capture of André. There were four other men, not named; hence I let Jock be one of them.

The Frasers are fictional, but like the people who actually lived in the Hudson Valley at the time. Oliver Cartwright is fictional, but his iron plantation is placed where the Courtland Furnace actually stood. Dick Conway is like many British runaway apprentices who became soldiers, deserted here, and eventually became Americans.

Printed in U.S.A.

FRASER'S FORGE